"I enthusiastically rec
personal devotion, sm
Roger S. Greenway m
powerfully doable."

- BARBARA YANDI
Founder of Hope for the Nations
Trainer for Student Volunteer Movement

"Obviously emerging from years of skilled angling, *Fish! The Call of the Master Fisher* covers a diamond's worth of facets that make up the mission challenge. With brevity and clarity Roger S. Greenway describes mission tasks, great and small, with striking examples from a variety of personal experiences in a variety of cultural contexts. Each chapter ends with relevant questions for ongoing reflection. Splashed liberally on every page, Greenway's joy in fishing for the Master is enticing and contagious for experienced and neophyte fishers of men and women. Its simplicity and directness make it an excellent tool for missionary orientation."

- ARIE C. LEDER
Senior Professor of Old Testament Studies
Calvin Theological Seminary
Veteran Missionary to Latin America

"Roger Greenway's passion for seeing people come to Christ is as vibrant today as it was when he and his wife arrived in Sri Lanka some fifty years ago. In this book he gives us tools to become fishers of men and women in North America and elsewhere. With discussion questions and action points at the end of each chapter, it is ideal for study groups in churches, mission organizations, and college classrooms. I will use it to enrich my students' learning in evangelism, church planting, and relationship building."

- GARY TEJA
Senior Director for the North, Central and South America.
The Bible League

"Fishing stories and basic evangelism are woven together in this unique and fascinating book. The author shares profound insights gained from years of fishing for fish and people. This makes the book educational as well as inspiring."

- MAURY DE YOUNG
Executive Director, Sportspersons Ministries International

To order additional copies of this book please contact:
Theophilus Publishing at gree@calvin.edu

The cost per book is $10 plus $5 shipping and handling
for orders of one to five books.
Discounts for larger quantities are available.

FISH!

FISH!

THE CALL OF THE MASTER FISHER

ROGER S. GREENWAY

Fish! The Call of the Master Fisher

Edited and produced by Perez Print Productions

Design and typesetting by Micah Ellis

Cover Design by Tobias Design

Printed in the United States of America

ISBN: 978-0-615-41657-1

Library of Congress Control Number: 2010940560

To all who answer the call of the

Master Fisher:

May your numbers grow,

your catch be great,

and God get all the glory.

CONTENTS

PREFACE

References to fish, fishing, and fishing boats are found throughout the biblical accounts of Jesus' ministry. It is not surprising, therefore, that fishing became a symbol of Jesus' work and the church's mission. When Jesus called four fishermen to be his first disciples, he knew that they would bring with them the traits and experiences of fishermen. Three years later he named them "apostles," fishers of men called to cast the gospel net in waters nearby and far away.

The thesis of this book is that fishing is a paradigm of Christian evangelism and missions. Just as Jesus' parables are often called "earthly stories with heavenly meanings," I regard biblical events involving fishing as "stories with evangelistic meaning." My two life-long passions, fishing for fish and fishing for men, have uncovered parallels and applications that led me to write this book. Permit me to remind readers who may feel that I carry the correspondence too far that it was Jesus himself who first drew the connection.

Why did I write the book? First of all, because I wanted to share my passion for both kinds of fishing and hopefully make it contagious. With that in mind I tell fish stories, all of them true of course, and the best of them drawn from my own experience. There are stories about big fish I landed and fish that got away, old fishing boats I tried to restore, and a Catholic nun who knew more about catching trout than most men ever learn (and she wrote a book about it). There's also a song about little boys who listen to God when they're fishing.

Second, I wrote this book to share ideas about fishing for fish and fishing for people. Experienced fishers love to talk and read about fishing because they know they can learn things from one another. Mission-minded Christians can also learn from those who've been involved in evangelism for a long time.

Third, I want to encourage Christians to make testifying for Jesus their mission in life. The title of this book is an imperative, *Fish!* It conveys a sense of urgency from the Master Fisher himself. Each of the twenty chapters closes with questions for individual reflection, group discussion, and personal response. Accountability questions keep readers "on the hook," confronting them personally with the call of Jesus.

Finally, I wanted to share bits and pieces of my own life experience in which the two kinds of fishing have been intertwined. Half a century ago, the Lord called me to become a fisher for him in distant parts of the world, and I tell the story of that call in the closing chapter. Yet long before I heard Christ call me, my maternal grandfather began teaching me to fish when I could barely hold a pole.

Exciting things are happening in the twenty-first century as the Spirit of God is raising up fishers all over the world. Many of them are from younger churches in places where, not long ago, Christians were few in number and often persecuted. In his or her own language and circumstances, each one hears the compelling call of the Master Fisher, "Follow me and you will catch people." And for them, especially, this book was written.

CHAPTER ONE

A Fisherman for Life

I am a fisherman for life.
I will always be a fisherman.
It's not something I do,
it is who I am.
Fishing is not an escape.
It is where I belong,
where I am supposed to be.
It is not a place,
but a lifelong journey
where I am supposed to be.
It is a passage my father showed me,
and that I will show others.
When you understand all of this,
you will know me,
and we will fish together.[1]

So says the Abu Garcia advertisement for quality fishing tackle. The words ripple through the minds of ardent sport fishers. It's how we are. We are fishermen for life. If we were orbiting a distant planet, we'd be looking for a lake with fish. It's what our parents taught us, and we pass it on to those we love. When you understand this, you know who we are.

The idea behind this book is that fishing is a paradigm for evangelism. We will see how truths about evangelism, examples,

1 *The Abu Garcia advertisement appeared in* In Fisherman: A Journal of Fresh Water Fishing, *February 1997.*

and models for spreading the gospel are woven into every aspect of fishing. We can learn more about evangelism from fishing than from any other work or pastime. For good reason, the first title the Bible gives to people who follow Jesus is "fishers of men." My goal is to echo Jesus' call and grow the company of fishers.

Jesus began his ministry by calling four men—Peter, Andrew, James, and John—to leave their family fishing business and follow him. By following Jesus they became fishers of men for life. Up until that time, their lives and livelihood had centered on fishing for fish. From that time on they fished for souls. The lessons learned during days and nights on the water were applied to evangelizing people. Fishers they would always be, but from that point on the "catch" would be different, and fishing would have a higher purpose.

The one who called them was Jesus, the Master Fisher. His Father had sent him to seek and to save the lost, and he passed on his mission to his followers. He said, "As the Father sent me, so I am sending you," and then he breathed on them his Spirit (John 20:21). The Holy Spirit was the divine outfitter who provided the equipment they needed. The training itself came from Jesus, who gave them patterns to follow. In this way Jesus turned professional fishers into fishers of men.

THE MASTER PLAN OF EVANGELISM

Among the many books written about evangelism, the most widely circulated is Robert E. Coleman's *The Master Plan of Evangelism.*[2] In the opening pages, Coleman raises a provoking question. He asks whether the multitude of activities carried on by Christians in the name of "evangelism" really fulfill Christ's commission to take the gospel to the whole world. The conclusion he reaches is, not really! He urges us to return to the simple plan that Jesus used and the way he taught his disciples by his own example. I call it the plan of the Master Fisher.

Fundamental to Jesus' plan was a focus on people instead of programs. Jesus invested his time and energy in committed people

2 *Robert E. Coleman,* The Master Plan of Evangelism. *Westwood, NJ: Fleming H. Revell, 1963. Many subsequent reprints.*

who would carry on the work of evangelism after he returned to heaven. For the most part, he called ordinary working-class men to enter into training under his personal direction. He would mold them into people who would move the world.

Jesus enjoyed no big "catches" during his three-year ministry on earth. The number of believers to whom he showed himself to be alive after the resurrection was about five hundred (1 Cor. 15:6). It did not bother Jesus that his initial catch was small. His goal was to reach the world, and his strategy was to concentrate his efforts on a few and make them leaders. Jesus believed that a small group, committed and trained, would train others and continue multiplying until the world was reached.

Fishing and Training Others to Fish

Coleman points out that Jesus taught primarily by close association and personal example. His disciples observed everything about him. They saw how he ministered to the few and to the multitudes. They heard his public teaching and private conversations. They observed how he responded to all kinds of people and situations: the blind, lame, and diseased pleading for healing; mature adults seeking answers to life's great questions; children and infants clamoring for attention; brokenhearted people pouring out their woes; public sinners and social outcasts. The disciples also saw how Jesus responded to bitter opposition and to the falling away of people who had followed him earlier.

Jesus fished continually. Even on the cross he evangelized, taking a repentant thief with him to paradise (Luke 23:39–43). As he fished, he trained others to fish. By listening and observing Jesus, the disciples learned evangelism.

What's Our Problem?

Why do most of us find it so hard to pass on the gospel to others? Can we show that our methods of "outreach" really are effective?

And are the ways we teach evangelism producing the results we want? What holds us back from following the simple approach of Jesus? Maybe we need to ask a prior question: How dare we separate being followers of Jesus from being fishers of men?

The Master Fisher is still calling men and women to his fishing school where skilled fishers teach the unskilled and the lesser skilled to follow experienced fishers until everyone is competent. It's a high calling, a lifelong journey. On it we learn to know the Great Fisherman better, and the importance of fishing together.

For Reflection, Discussion, and Action

1. *Describe the evangelism program of your church. Evaluate its effectiveness.*
2. *What hinders us from following Jesus' method? How can we overcome the barriers?*
3. *Where are you personally in the journey called "evangelism"? Where would you like to be? What steps are you ready to take to get there?*

Chapter 2

There Aren't Any Fish in This Pond

For some time I attended a church that had very little outreach to the people of its neighborhood. The members reasoned like this: "Around here, most people already have a church, so it's no use talking to them. The rest aren't interested in church, so talking to them is a waste of time, too."

When the annual church picnic came around, the church invited my wife and me to join them on a farm where they held the picnic every year. There was a large pond on the farm, and I asked if there were fish in the pond. "No," I was told. "Just frogs and weeds." Several chuckled when I took a fishing rod from my car. I could almost hear what they were thinking: "What does this crazy missionary think he's doing? There aren't any fish in this pond, as he'll soon find out. But the chuckling stopped when after a couple of casts, I landed a thirty-six-inch northern pike. The big fellow had been lying there in the weeds for years, probably chuckling to himself as one church picnic after another came and went without anyone trying to catch him.

I was struck by what I saw as a parallel between the church people's assumption that there weren't any fish in the pond and their skepticism over whether there were winnable people in the neighborhood. They doubted both, and hence tried neither! These were gracious, warmhearted Christians who meant well, but they had become so introverted that they'd lost the fisherman's spirit of adventure and faith.

Fishing in Strange Waters

Missionaries who go to other countries understand from the outset that they'll be fishing in strange waters at first. They'll have to learn and use a new language, develop new intercultural skills, and fish in new ways. There will be plenty of hurdles to overcome, and if they are not dead serious about Christ's call to go wherever he sends them, they probably won't last long.

The Lord doesn't call all of us to venture into unfamiliar places. He wants many of us to fish close to shore, which means in general North America where people have been familiar with Christianity for a long time. However, two major changes have occurred in America. The lake where we fish has changed, and it's caught us by surprise.

First, the ethos of American society has changed with respect to religion and the church. For many years church people felt safe and snug in a Christianity-friendly environment. Church services on the whole were well attended, children went to Sunday school, and mission budgets were met. Then, beginning in large cities, things started to change. The secularism that decades before had turned "Christian Europe" into a religious wasteland began to take hold in America. Some sections of the country moved down the road more rapidly than others, but none remained unaffected. Today, millions of Americans are biblically illiterate, and what they think they know about the Christian faith is confused to say the least. Whether we admit it or not, America has become a mission field from within.

Second, America was turned into a mission field from without. The changes in the immigration laws that were made in the mid-1960s opened the door to immigrants from all over the world. They impacted the religious profile of the United States more than any other piece of legislation in our nation's history. As a result, there is today an unprecedented number of differences in terms of languages, cultures, and religions. In major American cities, more than a hundred different languages are spoken in the homes of public school children. While visiting Chicago a while back, one of our granddaughters perceptively asked her parents, "Doesn't anybody here speak English?"

Along with the languages, different religions became part of the social fabric of North America. Churches in the city now stand between temples and mosques. Some of the temples and mosques may be better attended than the churches. American society has become a vast mosaic representing all the nations, cultures, and religions of the world.

Are There Fish in This Pond?

There are plenty of fish to be caught in the North American pond. Christians would do well to rejoice and praise God for providing us with marvelous opportunities to evangelize people of all nations, starting at our doorsteps. But most of us are not prepared for this. Cultural differences and prejudices from all sides are the lamentable barriers that hinder great things from happening.

Take, for example, a church I once knew very well in Grand Rapids, Michigan. Starting in the 1960s, the neighborhood around the church passed through one racial and cultural transition after another as newcomers arrived and traditional church members left. As hard as leaders and members fished, nothing worked and the church withered. Wisely, the remnant that was left voted to turn over the property to a vibrant Korean congregation that needed larger facilities. From day one this new congregation took the wise step of supplying earphones with audio translation for visitors who didn't understand the Korean language. Too bad the former congregation didn't do that.

During my years as a missionary pastor in Sri Lanka, the small island off the coast of India, I sometimes went fishing off the jetty in the Colombo harbor. I wasn't an expert at saltwater fishing, and the types of fish in the Indian Ocean were entirely strange to me. I used the bait that local fishers recommended and was amazed at the variety of fish I caught. Since most were new to me, I had to ask other fishers what they were called. But they were fish, and that was what I was after. Catching a new type of fish became the most exciting part of fishing.

This experience reflected my entire ministry in Sri Lanka. Before coming to the island, both my wife and I had grown up in churches that were largely mono-cultural. They consisted almost entirely of the same kind of "fish," which is to say the members spoke the same language, wore similar clothing, ate the same foods, and acted as respectable, middle-class Americans were expected to act. But life and ministry in metropolitan Colombo was very different. I served as senior pastor of three small congregations, each composed of people who spoke a different language and came from a different religious and cultural background. Our point of unity lay in the fact that all of us were drawn by the same Holy Spirit to worship the one Lord and Savior, Jesus Christ. The three groups shared the same church facilities, went out in teams to evangelize, and periodically held united worship services with translators. Our unity in Christ stood at the forefront of our witness.

For Reflection, Discussion, and Action

1. *When new fish appear in your pond, what is your reaction?*
2. *What can we do to overcome the mono-culturalism that grips so many of us?*
3. *Who are the new fish in the community? How will we reach them?*

CHAPTER 3

CATCH FISH OR DROWN WORMS

You find two kinds of fishers. First, there are fishers who simply "go fishing." They go mainly to have a good time, and in the process they drown worms. Fish or no fish, they come home happy. They say with a smile, "We went fishing."

Then there are those who go fishing with the serious intention of catching fish. They are not satisfied with merely being on the water and wetting the line. They intend to find the fish and outsmart them. These are serious fishers, and they bring home fish.

These two kinds of fishers can be easily identified. Observe their preparations. The first kind stops at a bait shop and buys whatever the salesperson suggests. They don't have any particular fish in mind—trout, bass, pike, or perch. Just fish. So any bait will do.

In contrast, serious fishers plan carefully. They know what they are after. They study the characteristics of different fish. They decide what kind of fish they are after and then choose their tackle and bait. Once they are on a lake or in a stream, they follow a course of action designed to catch fish.

Turning to evangelism, you find two kinds of Christians. The first kind talk a lot about "outreach," "growing the church," and "reaching out to one's neighbor." Yet they have only the foggiest notion of how to do it. They occasionally attract some people to their the church, more by accident than design, but the people don't stay long.

There are others who are intentional about evangelism. They seriously investigate the needs, aspirations, hurts, and misconceptions of unbelievers. They pray for, look for, and try to create opportunities to share the gospel. They are ready when opportunities open up.

Serious evangelists are constantly on the lookout for lost and hurting people. They equip themselves ahead of time by memorizing scriptures and forming answers to common questions. They go to places where lost people are likely to be found and put themselves in contact with them.

Intentional evangelists seek to master the art of leading people to Christ. They learn from whomever they can. When they meet new believers, they inquire as to who or what attracted them to the gospel. They do this because their purpose is to catch fish, not merely to "go fishing and drown worms." They are intent on learning every means the Spirit uses to draw people to Christ.

We are living today in a world of hungry fish. No generation in history has seen more people spiritually adrift, dissatisfied with their traditional religion, and wondering where they might find something better. This makes good weather for fishing. Lakes and streams are fuller than ever with hungry fish looking for food, ready to nibble, maybe to bite, and awaiting serious fishers.

A Lesson from the Master Fisher

The world in Jesus' day was similar to ours with respect to hungry fish. Jesus, the Master Fisher, taught powerful lessons in evangelism by the way he reached out to people of many kinds. One of those people was a rich tax collector named Zacchaeus. You find the story in Luke 19:1–10. Jesus was on foot and was entering the beautiful city of Jericho when he spotted Zacchaeus on the limb of a tree. Jesus called him to come down.

You would not normally expect a person like Zacchaeus to want to meet Jesus. Zacchaeus was a Jew who literally had "sold his soul" for the sake of money. He worked as a tax collector on behalf of the Romans whose army occupied Palestine. His job made him rich, but it also made him an outcast among his own people. People like Zacchaeus were hated by everyone. They could not attend worship because they were forbidden to enter the temple or synagogue. They were labeled "sinners," persons cut off from God and the covenant community.

There are many people like Zacchaeus alive today. They have grieved their families, destroyed their marriages, alienated their children, and forsaken God. In some cases they have ruined their health for the sake of prosperity and fun. But some of them are beginning to realize the futility of their material pursuits and the spiritual emptiness of their lives. The harm they've done to others now haunts them, and like Zacchaeus they are wondering if somehow they might change the direction of their lives. This is the moment when they need to meet Jesus. He specializes in changing lives.

Jesus, the Intentional Evangelist

Jesus spotted Zacchaeus through the protective foliage of the tree. When Zacchaeus heard Jesus call him by name, he must have been shocked. If Jesus knew who Zacchaeus was, he probably knew what kind of person Zacchaeus was as well. Surely, a holy man like Jesus would only condemn him. But he heard Jesus say, "I intend to stay at your house today." All excited, Zacchaeus scrambled down the tree to take Jesus to his house.

Jesus, the intentional evangelist, had eyes to see in an unexpected place a person whose spiritual life was a mess, but in whom God's Spirit had created a desire to be turned in a new direction. Jesus knew how to deal with a person like that. Jesus seized the opportunity and invited himself to this man's home. Before the day was over Zacchaeus was completely transformed.

The story ended with Jesus saying to his disciples, "The Son of Man came to seek and to save what was lost." That was their lesson for the day, and they never forgot it. They had seen what Jesus did and heard what he said about the intention of his ministry, which was to seek, find, and save lost people. Someday they would include the story of Zacchaeus in the book called the Bible, so that generations to come might learn from Jesus how to evangelize.

When we lived in Asia, I always carried gospel tracts in my pocket and distributed them freely. One day, I was talking to a wealthy Christian woman when a poor, lame beggar approached and asked me if I had something he could read. I was surprised that he was literate and gladly gave him a tract. As he hobbled away, the woman remarked, "You've just wasted a tract. He'll never become a Christian."

A few days later, who should appear at our door but this same beggar. He had hobbled halfway across the city to reach our house, and what he came for was something more to read. I gave him a copy of John's Gospel, and he sat near the house the rest of the day reading it. By evening he was asking what he had to do to become a Christian. That lame beggar became my Zacchaeus.

For Reflection, Discussion, and Action

1. *Whom can we identify right now who may be like Zacchaeus in the tree, a person wanting to know Jesus? What should we do to turn that person's desire into reality?*
2. *Given the number of fish we bring home, are we serious fishers or merely the kind that drown worms?*

Chapter 4

Think Like a Fish

I admire a certain high school teacher for two things: his ability to inspire kids to learn and his skills as a fisherman. Trout he's caught have broken state records. On icy cold days, when school is out you can see him in the river wearing waders and doing what he does so well, catching fish.

One day I asked him to tell me the secret of his success in catching fish and teaching kids. His answer went like this: I've fished all my life, and I apply all I know about fish to catching them. On a lake or in a river, I try to think like a fish. Then when I come to school, I try to think and feel the way the kids do. That's how I can get through to them.

He wasn't kidding. He has earned two advanced degrees in education, has published books on teaching, and often speaks at teacher conferences. Few people in our town know as much as he does about education and about kids. In the same way, as a fisherman he has learned all he can about fish, their habits and habitats, the foods they like or dislike, and how to catch them. What he knows about fishing is matched by what he understands about fish, and added up it makes him a master fisherman.

What Kind of Fish Is This?

By way of contrast, let me tell about a wealthy friend of mine who at the age of fifty decided he'd missed something important in life, namely, fishing. He flew to upstate New York and enrolled for a week of instruction at an upscale fishing academy. There the experts taught him to tie trout flies, how to use the best rods and reels money can buy, and wear all the right clothing for any kind of weather. He came home with all the gear to make him the "complete angler," with a certificate from the fishing academy to prove it.

My friend meant well, but after all they'd told him and sold him at the academy, he still had a problem: he knew scarcely anything about fish. His ignorance became embarrassingly clear when I offered to take him fishing on a Michigan lake. He needed twenty minutes to load all his fishing gear into the boat. I said nothing, but I knew that most of it would be useless. To get him started, I coaxed him away from the big lures he wanted to use to a simple hook, line, and sinker. In a few minutes he pulled up a bluegill, which is the most common species in Michigan lakes and easy to catch. Wearing a smile from ear to ear he held up the bluegill and asked, "What kind of fish is this?" I could hardly keep from laughing. He'd gone to school to learn fishing, and he'd invested a lot in tackle and lures. But he didn't know anything about fish. Even a small bluegill dangling on his line was a mystery to him.

Think again about the teacher, the master fisherman, who said that the secret of success lay in the fact that he "thought like a fish." He was using a figure of speech called hyperbole, which means employing exaggeration for the purpose of making a point. His point was that in his pursuit of becoming a skilled fisherman, he not only mastered the use of rods, reels, and lures, he also learned all he could about fish. By putting the two together, he achieved his purpose.

In his role as a teacher, he followed the same approach. He not only mastered the subjects he taught, he did his best to understand the kids—what they were thinking and looking for. Simply put, he tried to think like them in order to teach them and make a lasting impression on them.

Jesus-Style Evangelism

Hardly any two stories could better illustrate the difference between Jesus-style evangelism and the kind that many of us try to carry out. In the "School of Fishing" where Jesus is the headmaster, the curriculum looks like this: (1) learn all you can about Jesus; (2) learn to look for and understand people who need Jesus; and (3) learn to put into practice his passion for souls. Let's see how this might translate into our lives.

Take the Bible Seriously

From the Bible we acquire spiritual foundations, the essential things we need to believe and pass on to others. The primary author of the Bible is none other than God the Holy Spirit, and his purposes are clear. "All Scripture is God-breathed and is useful for teaching, rebuking, correcting and training in righteousness, so that the people of God may be thoroughly equipped for every good work" (2 Tim. 3:16–17). "Faith comes from hearing the message," wrote the apostle Paul, "and the message is heard through the word of Christ" (Rom. 10:17). In evangelism, there is no other legitimate "bait" than the good news about Jesus.

Always Be Looking for Unsaved, Unchurched, and Uncared-For People

Being a "neighbor" in the biblical sense means more than becoming acquainted with people who live or work nearby. It means drawing near to strangers, to people who are different than you, and to people who may need your help.

Check out what Jesus taught about this in Luke 10:33–37. Who proved to be the neighbor to the victim of violence by the side of the road? Applying this to ourselves means keeping our eyes open for strangers, immigrants, newcomers, people who are hurting, and anyone going through some kind of crisis. Pray that the Holy Spirit will lead you to such people and give you opportunities to show them Christ's love and mercy.

Years ago, an African-American evangelist taught me an important lesson about evangelism. "The birds you catch," he said, "are birds with broken wings." How true that is. Healthy birds fly away, while weak and injured birds get caught. Likewise, people in distress are often more open to the gospel. Everything else having failed them, they are open to the Savior. Keep your eyes open, discern people's needs, and show love wherever you can. Crises are often Holy Spirit-prepared openings to the hearts of lost people.

Share Gospel Truths, Answer Questions, and Watch God's Spirit Work

Look at how Jesus evangelized the Samaritan woman (John 4:1–26). Jesus reached out by asking her to do a favor, and he held out the gospel "bait" by telling her about water that would quench her thirst forever. To each of her questions, Jesus gave an answer, and each answer told her more about who he was. Here was the Master Fisher at work with a lost and hurting soul, and what began at a well spread to the whole town (John 4:39–42).

For Reflection, Discussion, and Action

1. *What are you doing to get to know unsaved, unchurched, and uncared-for people?*
2. *What crisis in your life can you use to build a bridge to some hurting person?*
3. *Accountability question: Whom will you look for this week; to whom you will be a true neighbor and by your deeds and words proclaim Christ?*

Chapter 5

The Pike That Got Away

On the wall of a barbershop in a midwestern town hung the mounted head of a large northern pike with two battered fishing lures caught in its mouth. Besides the lures, a large hook was stuck in its jaw. The fish's head wasn't the largest on the barbershop wall, but it caught the most attention and prompted the most conversation. As a boy, I didn't mind waiting for a haircut as long as there were men in the shop talking about fishing.

One day, the pike with lures in its mouth was the particular subject of discussion. Several fishermen commented that the lures were similar to lures they'd lost when their lines broke. Excitedly, they described the battles they'd fought with pike the size of this one. Might this be the very fish that years before had broken their lines and gotten away?

Speculation like this led to discussions about the strength of fishing lines they used. Some said they preferred to cast with ten-pound test line, while others argued that for pike they preferred much stronger line, up to twelve-, fourteen-, or eighteen-pound test. Everyone expressed concern about losing fish, and this led to discussions about the ways fishing lines could be damaged. Weak spots in the line may have been the reason that the pike on the wall so often got away. This led to questions about how often fishermen should replace their lines or try the new and better ones that were advertised. Among fishermen, discussions like this never end.

One thing they all agreed upon was that northern pike were born with an arsenal of tricks on how to get away. Sometimes pike take the lure with hardly a jerk, and you can't be sure whether you have weeds on the line or a fish. Then all at once they lash this way and that, dive to the bottom and get tangled in the weeds, defying you to pull them to the boat. Even the best lines can't take that kind of strain too long, and when lines break fish get away.

After many escapes, the fish on the barber shop wall had been hooked on line that didn't break. That brought to a close its days of defiance. The battered hooks and lures in its mouth bore witness to its strength and cleverness. But in the end he was caught.

Evangelism in the Twenty-First Century

I find in the barbershop story an analogy to what I believe will be a major challenge to evangelism in the twenty-first century. Many churches are in crisis because they have lost so many of their young adults, and they wonder if they'll retain the youth who still attend. In some cases, it's a matter of young adults deciding to change churches or denominations. In other cases, they feel that church is no longer important to them and doesn't fit their chosen lifestyle.

The trend away from church began in Europe several decades ago and now is spreading in North America. From rural communities to urban centers, among Catholics and Protestants, conservative churches and mainline, the absence of young adults is a serious problem. I'm not singling out so-called "marginalized" youth, the school dropouts, street kids, drug addicts, and gang members. They certainly must be reckoned as people outside the church, but they aren't the only ones. I'm thinking about young adults in their twenties and thirties who come from middle-class Christian homes, drop out of church, change their religious and moral lifestyle, bewilder their parents, and frustrate Christian leaders.

Parents and pastors together have learned to identify with the father in Christ's parable of the prodigal son. The heartbroken father must have asked a thousand times, "What did I do wrong? What made this child on whom I poured instruction and love go off as he did? Now he's beyond my reach, and all I can do is wait and pray. Maybe someday he'll come home." And home he came, as the parable says, but only after admitting he'd made a painful mistake, followed bad advice, and discovered for himself that the world's allurements were hollow.

No family or church has ever been perfect, and there have always been conditions that might trigger a son or daughter's rebellion. All parents have things to repent of, and we should. But we must recognize the influence of the culture in which young adults have been raised. It is a culture that places very little value on religious and moral truth. It insists on freedom-of-choice for everyone, and everything's okay if it suits you. That is the world in which twenty-first-century evangelism is carried on. It means witnessing to Christ among people who don't remember Christian hymns, Bible verses, or the gospel message.

Recently I spoke to a man in his early forties whom I knew was raised in a godly home. I asked where he attended church. With a shrug he replied, "Nowhere! I've moved beyond all that." With a look of self-confidence he described his successful business, how he enjoyed the best that life offers, and felt no need for either God or the church. With a grin he added, "I've sure got better things to do on weekends."

He did his best to project the image of a happy secularist. Yet I detected, and I pray that I wasn't mistaken, hints of things that didn't fit the picture. My gut feeling is that like the prodigal in Christ's parable, this man remembers the Father's house and things in his childhood that now are missing. Like embers still glowing, those memories may one day be breathed on by the Spirit of God and made to burst into flame. Somehow, somewhere, the Great Fisherman may cast a lure to him, and the tough old rebel won't get away.

For Reflection, Discussion, and Action

A devotional book I often use encourages praying for church members who "got away." I find the following to be highly relevant to twenty-first-century evangelism:

- *Pray that in our families we will forgive one another for past sins, including abuse of any kind.*

- *Ask God to restore broken relationships and bring wholeness to our households and circles of friends.*
- *Pray that the members of our churches will have eyes to see lost people who, for whatever reason, at one time left the fold.*
- *Ask God's Spirit to give us a forgiving spirit and a nonjudgmental attitude toward those who by God's grace are returning home.*
- *Pray that God will make us reconcilers and restorers in all our relationships and give us the humble courage such work requires.*
- *Pray that people around us may see Jesus Christ shining through us.*
- *Ask God to use us to draw back to him the lost who strayed away and win the lost who never before heard the gospel.*[1]

After reflection and discussion spend time in prayer for yourself and others.

1 *Adapted from* Patterns for Prayer: 52 weeks of prayer ideas. *Grand Rapids, MI: CRC Publications, 1995.*

Chapter 6

Are Some Fish Too Small?

There was once a boy who lived near a lake, and the boy loved to fish. He would sit for hours with his cane pole and can of earthworms, and he caught a lot of fish. Most of them were perch and sunfish, and almost all of them were small. Proudly, he took the fish home for his family to eat. But because he was very young, his father had to clean the fish his son caught.

After a while, the father got tired of cleaning little fish. He cut a stick to a certain length and said to his son, "From now on, don't keep any fish shorter than this stick. Small fish are a lot of trouble to clean, and they don't provide us much to eat. So from now on only come home with bigger ones."

The boy stared at the stick and his heart sank. He knew that most of the fish he brought home were much shorter than the stick. To make matters worse, his father tied a larger hook to his line, a hook too large for small fish to be caught on. The young fisherman liked to catch fish whether they were big or small, but from now on the small ones weren't to be "keepers."

Are Young Children "Keepers"?

Jesus' answer to this question was a loud, Yes! On one occasion, when the disciples of Jesus tried to shoo little children away, Jesus rebuked them sharply. It happened when Jesus was on his way to Jerusalem where his enemies waited to kill him. Along the road, mothers who loved Jesus were bringing their children for Jesus to bless them, but the disciples tried to prevent the children from coming. Jesus called the children to him and said,

Let the little children come to me, and do not hinder them, for the kingdom of God belongs to such as these. I tell you the truth, anyone who will not receive the kingdom of God like a little child will never enter it. (Luke 18:16–17)

Here we see Jesus, who is the perfect revelation of God, showing the heart of God for children. These words and actions of Jesus stamped Christianity as a religion ardently pro-children. This comes from the fact that Jesus loves children and wants to bless them. Over the years, no other religion has come close to matching the concern of Christians for the needs of children.

Anyone who knows children knows they have many kinds of needs. They need food, shelter, clothing, and protection. Children have emotional needs, too. They need love from people who care about them and in whom they can trust. Children need to be taught and educated. They need guidance and discipline. "Special needs" children have all these and more. They require special care, therapy, and an abundance of patience and love.

Most important of all, children need to be told about God and his Word. They need to be brought to Jesus for his blessing and salvation. The circumstances in which children grow up may vary greatly, but there is not a child in the world that does not need the Lord Jesus. Jesus did say, "Let the children come to me." Reflect on this, and on the fact that more than 80 percent of the world's children and youth grow up in non-Christian societies where it's unlikely they'll learn about Jesus.

How Did Jesus Look upon Children?

First of all, Jesus viewed children as image-bearers of God. As the eternal Son of God, Jesus was there when the triune God said, "Let us make man [male and female] in our image . . ." (Gen. 1:26). He took part creating human nature, which is different from the nature of all other earthly beings. Human beings have the capacity to know God, enjoy God's fellowship, work for him, and consciously worship him. For that reason, when Jesus saw people bringing children to him, it made his heart glad. He took them in his arms and blessed them. This was the way it was meant to be from the beginning of the world.

Second, Jesus saw how vulnerable children are to abuse, violence, temptations, and wrong ideas. Jesus knew that getting at children and youth has always been Satan's favorite strategy. Satan's major goal is to prevent children from knowing and serving God. If he fails to kill them in the womb by abortion, or soon after birth by infanticide, Satan tries other things. He fills them with wrong ideas, hurts them emotionally, damages their bodies and minds, sears their consciences, and ultimately destroys them if he can. If we heard all the gruesome things that Satan does against children, it would be more than we could take.

Jesus knew all this, and he stressed the importance of someone intervening to bring little ones to him. He saw beyond the particular children that mothers were bringing to him that day and saw the millions of children who never have a chance to hear of God's saving love unless somebody makes a special effort to reach them and tell them about Jesus.

The Saddest Sight I've Seen

When I was a missionary-pastor in Sri Lanka, nothing made me sadder than the sight of mothers teaching children to pray before statues of the Buddha at the temple near our home. I always thought of the first two commandments, where God says that we should worship him and him alone (Ex. 20:3–4). The sad fact is that throughout the world, countless children learn from infancy to worship idols. Others are taught that there is no God at all. Is there anything more important than reaching out to such children with the gospel?

In his preaching, Charles H. Spurgeon often appealed directly to the children in his audience. He urged them to put their faith in Jesus and assured them that Jesus loved them and cared for their souls. In his book, *Come Ye Children*, Spurgeon urges adult believers to use every possible means to teach children the basic truths of the Bible. He points out that humility, trust, and dependence are childhood's distinguishing traits. Christ's kingdom, Spurgeon concludes, is composed exclusively of children and childlike persons of all ages who humbly trust Jesus to save them and meet their needs. "None find entrance there," he says, "except they receive the gospel as a little child receives it."[1]

Since that is true, and good fishers copy Jesus, attention to children should play a major role in our "fishing." To Jesus, no fish is too small.

For Reflection, Discussion, and Action

1. *In the children's program of your church, what percentage of the children come from homes where the parents are not practicing Christians? What can you do to increase the percentage?*
2. *Alongside churches, there are evangelistic organizations designed especially to reach children from unchurched homes. How much support do you and your church give to such organizations? Can you do better?*
3. *One of the great "fathers" of the church, Clement of Alexandria, wrote, "Faithful Christians copy Christ." List some ways to copy Christ in what we do for children.*

1 *C.H. Spurgeon,* Come Ye Children. *Pasadena, TX: Pilgrim Publications, n.d., 43.*

Chapter 7

Fishers Who Don't Fish

The story is old, but it strikes me every time I hear it. It's an allegory about a group of people who called themselves "fishermen." They lived in a land that had many streams and lakes filled with hungry fish. Week after week, month after month, and year after year these fishermen came together in meetings and talked about fishing. They celebrated the abundance of fish nearby and discussed how they might go about catching them. They carefully defined and redefined what fishing meant. One of their favorite slogans was, "Fishing is the primary task of every fisher."

These people built costly clubhouses for their weekly meetings. They sponsored nationwide conferences and even worldwide congresses to discuss theories of fishing and the best baits, methods, and boats for fishing. They organized themselves with boards and committees and appointed directors. They built a large and beautiful "Fishing Headquarters" where the main job was to promote the goal that "everyone should be a fisher and every fisherman should fish." But one thing they themselves did not actually do: they didn't fish.

Their zeal for fishing led them to form a special agency designed to send out fishermen to faraway lakes where there were more fish. The agency's task was to promote the idea of fishing, recruit new fishers, and keep the vision of fishing before the members of the local fishing clubs. In the course of time, the agency organized training programs to teach new fishers how to fish. Seminars were offered on the theory of fishing, the needs of fish, where to find fish, the best baits for different fish, and how to present the baits effectively to catch more fish. The people who led the seminars had doctorates in fishology and were regarded as experts in fishing. But these teachers themselves didn't fish. They only taught fishing and wrote books about it.

Every year more people graduated from fishing schools and were given fishing degrees and licenses. Some were sent to engage in full-time fishing in distant waters that were known to be filled with fish. Far from home, they studied the cultures of the various fish and the history of fishing in particular waters. They went to see the places where great fishers had caught fish in centuries past. They praised those fishers of yore, wrote books about them, and studied the record of how they became so successful in fishing. But one thing they did not do themselves—they didn't fish.

In their enthusiasm for fishing, the fishermen published fishing magazines, fishing guides, and fishing books that analyzed the different kinds of fish around the world. Printing presses were kept busy day and night producing materials devoted to fishing methods, fishing boats, motors, and other equipment, the proper clothing fishermen should wear, and the psychology of fish. A speakers' bureau was organized to schedule special speakers on the subject of fishing.

All this busy activity produced results. Many responded to the call to become fishermen. They were examined, commissioned, and sent to fish in distant waters. But like the fishermen back home, they engaged in all kinds of good activities that did not directly relate to catching fish. Some spent their time visiting fish hatcheries and discussing the best way to raise fish in ponds. Others said they liked being part of a fishing party, but their gifts were more in line with furnishing fishing equipment to others. Quite a number preferred to be administrators and spent their lives overseeing the vast number of activities involved in the fishing enterprise.

After one stirring meeting on "The Necessity of Fishing," one young fellow left the meeting and went fishing. The next week he reported that he had caught some very large fish. The fishermen honored him for his excellent catch and scheduled him to visit all their big meetings to tell how he had done it. He became so busy telling about his experience that he no longer had time for fishing. Nevertheless, he was elected to the Fishermen's General Board and was praised for his leadership in the great work of fishing.

The sacrifices that some of the fishermen made cannot be overlooked. They put up with a variety of difficulties. Some lived near polluted water and bore the smell of dead fish every day. Some focused on fishing club members who had lost interest in fishing and were delinquent in attending the weekly meetings. Others put up with ridicule coming from people who said fishing was unfair to fish and potentially harmful to the environment. Hardest to bear were questions such as: If you are fishermen, why don't you fish? Are you following the master fisher, when all you do is talk, write, organize programs, and hold meetings, without ever really fishing?[1]

For Reflection, Discussion, and Action

1. *How does the story make you feel? Why?*
2. *What pieces in the story seem to be especially applicable to us?*
3. *If following Jesus involves actually "fishing" for lost people, what specific things should we start doing? List the steps and when you will do them.*

1 *The story is attributed to Pastor John M. Drescher of the Scottdale Mennonite Church, Scottdale, Pennsylvania. It is adapted here from the form in which it appeared in* People Sharing Jesus *by Darrell W. Robinson, Nashville, TN: Thomas Nelson Publishers, 1995: 21-23.*

Chapter 8

Fisherwomen

Prepare yourself for surprises! Did you know that the first book published in the English language was printed by William Caxton in 1487? That was before Columbus discovered America. The second book in the English language was printed a few years later. It was called the Book of St. Albans, and it contained the "Treatise on Fishing with an Angle." [1]

Isn't it amazing that one of the first books published in English contained a section about fishing? Yet that's only part of the story. The section on fishing was written not by a fisher man, but by a fisher woman. Her name was Juliana Barnes. She apparently came from a noble family and was the prioress of the Sopwell Nunnery in Sopwell, England.[2] She was a nun I would like to meet!

Over the years, most of the books and articles about fishing have been written by men. The all-time classic was a book by Izaak Walton. It was titled *The Compleat Angler,* and it appeared in 1653. Walton's book on fishing was reprinted fifty times before a second printing appeared of the King James version of the Bible. There must have been a great number of ardent fishers in "merry old England."

In her writing, Sister Juliana showed that she not only knew a lot about fishing, particularly trout fishing, but she also was able to blend her ideas about fishing as a sport with her religious piety and moral standards. Listen to her advice about trout fishing:

1 *"Angle" is an old English word referring to hook-and-line fishing. Hence, an "angler" is a person that fishes with hook and line. "Angle worms" are earthworms used for bait in angling.*

2 *The information about Juliana Barnes' book is from Justin Isherwood, "The Great She,"* In-Fisherman, *Oct.-Nov., 2001: 72-73.*

The trout is really fine fish to eat and it's also a great fighter on the line. The trout is at home wherever you find a clean gravel bottom in streams. Fish for trout in March by hanging a minnow on your hook by its lower lip.

In April use lamprey and cankerworms for bait. In May take stoneflies and grubworms from under cow turds. In June take earthworms and nip off their heads. In July use big red worms, in August house flies, in September earthworms and minnows. Do the same in October, for earthworms and minnows are special for trout in all seasons. From April to September the trout leap, and I advise you to angle for them with artificial flies appropriate to each month.

The following baits hold up well on your hook: Flour and lean meat from the hips of a rabbit or cat, virgin wax, and sheep's fat. Crush them fine in a mortar, mix over a fire with a little purified honey, make into little balls and bait your hook.

Juliana, the fishing nun, leaves us no doubt about her detailed acquaintance with the art of trout fishing in her day. Now hear her give ethical and religious advice in connection with fishing:

In going about your sport, don't damage anyone's hedges, don't trespass in any poor man's private water without first getting his permission. If you open a gate, shut it behind you. Don't use the sport of fishing for selfish gain or making money, but only for your enjoyment and health, and most importantly for your soul. When you go fishing, don't take a lot of people with you, for they will detract you from communing with God.[3]

Women in Evangelism

Women played important roles in evangelism and church development in the days of the apostles. See how many names of women are mentioned by Paul in Romans 16. Paul refers to women who "worked very hard" and in some cases "risked their lives." Paul and the churches he planted were grateful for the women as well as the men who gave themselves unreservedly for the spread of the gospel.

3 *The updated English is mine, RSG..*

Much has been written about the things men have done in missions, and it is undeniable they have done a great deal. But if you dig a bit you discover a vast number of women, some of them single and others married, who made enormous contributions to the growth of Christ's church around the world. In the nineteenth and twentieth centuries, foreign missions gripped the hearts of hundreds of thousands of women in England and North America. Missions enlisted their prayers, energies, financial support, and leadership. Women read mission literature, and organized mission prayer meetings and mission societies. They engaged in frontline mission service at home and abroad. To this day, most checks written in support of missionaries are checks signed by women.

In the work of personal evangelism, women often excel over men. I've never met a woman the likes of Juliana Barnes, who knew so much about catching fish in her country's lakes and streams. But I've known women in evangelism, especially at the level of local congregations, who are simply unsurpassed. This should not surprise us, because women in general possess gifts that are highly important in evangelism, such as conversing easily with neighbors, welcoming newcomers, and developing friendships. Since so much of personal evangelism has to do with becoming a friend and building relationships, women who fish for souls are blessings from God.

For Reflection, Discussion, and Action

1. *Think of the new people who recently joined your church. Who were more instrumental in drawing them to church and making them feel at home, women or men? How did they do it? What can we learn from them?*
2. *Juliana Barnes showed great respect for nature (don't break any one's hedge), for property rights (don't trespass without permission), and for fish conservation (don't catch more than you need). How can we show similar concerns?*
3. *For Juliana, communing with God was part of fishing. Suggest some ways in which you might enjoy outdoor activities and at the same time draw closer to God.*

CHAPTER 9

"HYPE" AND A FISHER'S TACKLE BOX

There is something almost sacred about a fisher's tackle box. Last Father's Day, my grandsons gave me a new box. It's the fifth I've had in my lifetime, and I fondly remember each one of them. The first came as a gift on my fifth birthday. It was a small box made of wood and painted green. Inside were hooks and sinkers of different sizes, a spool of black braided line, two bobbers, and a few lures. One of the lures was a gift from an uncle who had carved it by hand.

My next two tackle boxes were larger, made of metal, and each of them lasted a couple of decades. I still have one of them, and though it's banged up, I don't have the heart to throw it away. After the metal boxes, I bought a large tackle box made of fiberglass. It had plenty of space for the hundred or more "indispensable" lures and other tackle I'd acquired, but it couldn't stand rough treatment, and it began to crack. It was replaced by the fifth box, and I hope this box lasts as long as I'm fishing.

Besides what's in my tackle box, I have all sorts of lures, reels, and other gear scattered around my office and garage. Thanks to my wife's forbearance, on a living room wall I have three display cases containing eighty of my all-time favorite lure, the Shakespeare Swimming Mouse. The number and variety of my lures tells one thing about me: that I've been a sucker for fishing hype for a long time.

FISHING HYPE

Look at fishing magazines, catalogs, and newspaper ads, and what do you see?

"Catch HUGE MUSKIES!"

"Slammin' SUPER SALMON"

"The Hottest Thing for SMALLMOUTHS!"

"Find WALLEYES Fast!"

Hype, hype, hype sells rods, reels, lures, boats, motors, and every conceivable type of fishing gear. Hype artists create illusions that we fishers can't ignore. Fishers are eternal optimists. We can fish for hours without catching anything and yet be sure that the next cast will net us a big one. The mere picture of a fish gets us excited. When fishers read about a new lure, a better line, or a smoother reel, wild illusions seize us. Our hands feel the pull of a fish so large it defies belief. We see our rod arched by the fish's weight with that new lure we need to buy protruding from its mouth. Nonfishers may laugh and say we're gullible, but fishers don't change, and advertisers know that well. Hype is what fills our tackle boxes.

Mission Hype

There is a type of hype that I call "mission hype." You find it wherever outreach programs are promoted by flamboyant slogans, exaggerated reports, and "miracle" stories. In the 1990s, a group in North America promised its supporters that if they'd donate enough money, the group would "finish the job of evangelizing the world by AD 2000." To the best of my knowledge, the goal wasn't reached.

Some people justify mission hype by pointing out that hype successfully raises money for good causes, and at the same time it makes donors feel good. Hype artists sound so pious that it's embarrassing to raise questions about the reports they present and the promises they pitch. But isn't it interesting that Jesus never used hype to promote his work? He didn't glamorize the miracles he performed, how many people he'd fed, or how he walked on water. Nor did he attempt to motivate his disciples by building inflated expectations. Instead, he talked to them about crosses they'd have to bear and opposition they'd face. He never once manipulated anyone for financial support.

Jesus knew that fishing for men was not going to be fun and

games. To the contrary, it would cost blood, sweat, and tears. Surely, there would be exhilarating times when sinners repented, and submitted their lives to God, and new churches were started. But along the way there would also be Satanic resistance and sometimes brutal persecution. When Jesus walked along the Sea of Galilee and called the four fishermen to be his disciples, he called them to take risks and make sacrifices. One of the four, James the son of Zebedee, would be beheaded by King Herod before his work of fishing for men had barely started. James was called to fulfill his mission by the witness of martyrdom (Acts 12:2).

Not Hype, but Commitment

When it comes to moving God's people to bearing witness for him and supporting the work of evangelism, it's not hype we need but straightforward calls for commitment. Hype is hollow, and using it to promote God's kingdom becomes a cover-up for shallow discipleship.

The twenty-first century is not going to be an easy time for Christian witness. As I see the global picture, two things stand out: first, more people are following Jesus than ever before, and churches are multiplying in places where not too long ago there were no churches at all. That leads me to conclude that the twenty-first century is likely to be the greatest time for spreading the gospel the church has ever seen. But I also see storm clouds ahead. Second, as the gospel spreads, opposition will intensify. Followers of non-Christian religions will cause more and more trouble for followers of Jesus Christ. Meanwhile salesmen for pluralistic religious views will infiltrate schools, intimidate politicians, and increase their power in the media.

More ominous still is the subtle erosion within many churches of conviction about basic teachings of Scripture. More and more people who claim to be Christians hesitate to affirm that Jesus is the only way to salvation. When convictions of that nature give way, other things soon tumble. Evangelism and missions make no sense if Jesus is only one way among many.

The days ahead will require more than hype to stir and maintain support for the Great Commission. It will take firm faith, deep commitment, a willingness to sacrifice even life itself, and unshakable loyalty to the one who calls, “Follow me and I will make you fishers of men.”

For Reflection, Discussion, and Action

1. *In what ways are fishing hype and mission hype similar?*
2. *Why will it require more than hype to maintain support for missions and evangelism in the twenty-first century?*
3. *Reflect on Acts 20:24, and answer the following question: Should the Lord call me, would I be willing to dedicate my life to spreading the gospel in a place where sanitation is poor, there are no sports I enjoy nor TV, Christians are few and often persecuted, I would have to raise my own support, and I might not know the results of my work until I get to heaven?*

CHAPTER 10

FISH FINDERS

Fish finders are fun to use. For a few hundred dollars, fishers can equip their boats with electronic devices that show on a screen the depth and temperature of the water, the shape of the bottom, the number of fish in the area, and at what depth the fish are swimming. Information like that removes some of the guesswork from fishing.

To say that 10 percent of the fishers catch 90 percent of the fish is probably an exaggeration. Just the same, fishers armed with fish finders have a better chance. Once you know where the fish are, you can adjust your lures, the depth of your lines, and the techniques you follow. Those things put together often lead to a bigger catch. But remember one thing: even the best fish finder can't make fish bite.

In evangelism it is important to know where people are in terms of their relationship to God and his Word. Some don't even know the basic teachings of the Christian faith, while others know quite a bit. With some, you can use biblical vocabulary and they will understand what you mean. Others, however, have only a shallow acquaintance with religious words and ideas, and you have to begin at the most elementary level.

Some years ago, James Engel, an expert on Christian communication, popularized a simple way to illustrate the challenge of evangelizing people at various "distances" from the gospel.[1] He developed what became known as the "Engel scale," and it goes like this: People who are far away from Christianity and hostile to it appear on the scale as being –7. These are people imbedded in some other religion

1 *James F. Engel,* Contemporary Christian Communication: Its Theory and Practice. *Nashville, TN: Thomas Nelson, 1979: 46ff.*

or regard themselves to be atheists. Witnessing to them requires much time and patience. A lot of preliminary teaching has to be done before they begin to understand what the gospel is all about.

At the same time, you find other people that have a fair amount of awareness of Christianity. Maybe they attended Sunday school when they were children and learned some Bible verses and songs. Or perhaps they had godly grandparents who talked to them about Jesus. You rate them as –6, –5, or even –4. Still others show evidence of a growing sense of their need for the gospel. They're confused about many things, but they know they are sinners and need a Savior, and you address them at that level. We'd say that on the Engel scale they can be rated as –2 or –1.

Persons at that point possess enough understanding of the gospel to make a responsible decision for or against Jesus Christ. Were they further back on the scale at –7, –5, or –4, asking them to receive Christ by faith would not make sense. They would not even know what you were talking about and might never want to talk about religion again. But when your spiritual fish finder tells you that people are hungry for Christ and the Holy Spirit has led them to nibble or more, set the "hook." Don't let those souls get away.

Mistakes We Make

Engel contends that Christians often make the mistake of talking to everyone as though they were all in the –3 to –1 zone. But multitudes aren't yet there. They have only vague notions about Christianity and are not prepared to respond to a gospel invitation. The wise witness will be cautious, sensitive to their religious feelings, and gently cast the gospel line without chasing them away.

I've preached in villages in Asia where no one knew who Jesus was. On the Engel scale, they were at –7, or less. If I wanted to communicate to them, I had to tailor my words carefully so that they might understand. In such places I generally began by telling about the one true God who created the world. He is a holy and mighty God, the only God that we ought to worship. Then I would tell them some stories about Jesus, why he came into the world, the miracles he did, how he died on a cross, and how he arose from the dead three days later. I'd let them ask me questions about Jesus and what he means to me. Finally, I would introduce them to a Christian from their area who would visit them again and tell them more. An immediate call for decision in such circumstances would not be wise. A lot of work had to be done to bring them from where they were at –7 to –6, –4, –2, and then by God's grace, decision time would come and some of them would respond.

You don't have to go to some remote area of the world to find people who know little about Christianity. Some of them are our neighbors, classmates, and fellow workers. What this means is that while non-Christians are all alike in their need for new birth, they differ so far as their ability to understand what we're talking about when we witness to them. Therefore, the wise evangelizer, like a fisher with a fish finder, will search around, learn as much as possible about people's religious backgrounds, and avoid the mistake of assuming too much too soon.

How the Spirit Works

As a fisher of men, I've done my own informal research over many years and in different parts of the world. My approach has been to discover how the Holy Spirit works in convicting sinners and drawing them to Christ (John 16:8–9). Everywhere I go I ask new believers how and under what circumstances they came to know and believe in Christ. After listening to many fascinating accounts, I have concluded that the Holy Spirit generally begins his saving work in people's hearts years before they consciously embrace Christ by faith. In many cases, the Spirit set the stage for their salvation before they were even born.

I've been told stories of long spiritual journeys full of strange twists and turns. Many different people had roles in the stories, and each contributed in some way to the outcome. Journeys to faith may begin in murky ignorance, sin, and rebellion, and in the early stages (–7, –6, –5) people are unaware of what is happening to them. If pressed too early to decide for Christ, the process can be stalled for a time. But the Spirit, whom the Bible describes as moving in mysterious ways, keeps the process going and brings them eventually to the conviction that they need forgiveness, that the gospel is true, and that Jesus Christ is the Savior they want as their own.

Recent stories out of China reinforce these conclusions. In many instances, young Chinese who were reared in rigid atheism at home and in school, and only recently became Christians, tell of grandparents who believed in Jesus and who years ago taught them things from the Bible. Those Chinese grandparents were fishers for Christ in secret, telling their grandchildren about Jesus despite threats and prohibitions. Now decades later, the Spirit is using the memories of their witness to lead their grandchildren to Christ. And the catch is larger than anyone could have imagined.

For Reflection, Discussion, and Action

1. *How does the Engel scale help us to present the gospel in an appropriate manner?*
2. *Describe three of your unsaved neighbors in terms of the Engel scale.*
3. *What are some ways to witness to them that might be effective?*
4. *Write down those neighbors' names and pray for them now and each day for a month.*

CHAPTER 11

OLD FISHING BOATS

When I was a teenager, I reconditioned several old fishing boats. They were wooden boats made by hand before World War II. They had been discarded by previous owners who regarded them as too old and leaky. In one case, an owner simply wanted something new and faster, and he was happy to let me take the old boat off his hands for free.

My friends did not understand my affection for old fishing boats. Aluminum boats had become popular by then, followed by fiberglass, which put wooden hulls out of style. But to me, there was something about the graceful lines of the old boats, the grain of the wood, and the way they handled in the water that newer boats couldn't match. Besides, there were memories associated with the old boats—memories of fishing trips, happy hours spent with fellow fishers, and of small boys learning to row the heavy oars. New boats don't bring back memories.

I remember one boat in particular because it had such beautiful lines. Not a boat made today has lines like that. It must have been a beauty when it was new. I wanted so much to see it glide across the water again that I invested a great deal of time, energy, and pocket money trying to save it. But the boat was beyond repair. The wood was too far gone. With a heavy heart I towed the old boat to a deep spot in the lake, loaded it with cement blocks, and with a private farewell ceremony, let it sink to the bottom.

OLD BOATS AND OLD CHURCH BUILDINGS

Old church buildings are often like old fishing boats. They have splendid architecture, beautiful stained glass windows, and most of all, precious memories of the saints who first met the Lord and worshiped there. But as with old fishing boats, it takes an enormous amount of money and effort to maintain aging church buildings. Roofs leak, plumbing breaks down, pipe organs cost a mint to repair, and everywhere you look there's something that needs fixing. Furthermore, when the buildings no longer serve the needs of people in the neighborhood, the upkeep doesn't seem practical. It is then that congregations have to decide what to do with the old buildings.

In large cities like New York, Chicago, Detroit, and dozens of other places across America, any number of churches have closed or changed hands. Starting in the 1950s, large numbers of city people migrated to the suburbs, leaving long-cherished church buildings empty. Complicating matters still further, new highways were built that divided traditional neighborhoods and isolated churches from their members. As a result, fine buildings became obsolete and no longer served the needs of their owners.

Some of the grandest church buildings in American cities belong to the Roman Catholic Church. But wave after wave of Catholics, like their Protestant counterparts, left the cities for the suburbs. The consequence is that in many old city neighborhoods, magnificent nineteenth-century sanctuaries stand like ghosts from the past, with no one using them. On a recent trip to Chicago I visited a parish church and its adjoining Catholic school buildings and residences for priests and nuns. All the buildings are now boarded up, their premises abandoned and prey to vandals.

"It's sad," commented an elderly nun who had spent most of her life teaching at the school and worshiping in the church. "But we must remember that buildings are merely material things. They are blessings to us for a certain length of time and then things change. We must keep in mind that buildings are inanimate, and we can't afford to maintain buildings that no longer are of use to us." The nun was right. Like old fishing boats, most old churches eventually must go down.

New Life through Changing Hands

Yet demolition is not the only option, nor the best. Let me illustrate this. The Reformed Church in America is the oldest Protestant denomination in America. In the early part of the twentieth century, the RCA had a dozen thriving congregations in the city of Philadelphia. My wife and I lived in Philadelphia near a magnificent gray stone church building on Broad Street. Its cornerstone still identified it as having been erected by the RCA. But by 1970, most of the traditional church members had moved away and the building was turned over to an African-American congregation that could immediately fill the auditorium. New life came to the old building by changing hands.

In 1984, the last RCA congregation within the city limits of Philadelphia closed down, and its building was sold to a Hispanic church that had outgrown its prior facilities. Within days new life could be seen in the old building, for it was again in the hands of Christians who lived in the neighborhood and would make the place their social and spiritual center. The transfer of the building to fellow believers who needed it made it a blessing to another generation of God's children.

Such transfers, however, are not easy. We love our old buildings, especially for the memories associated with them. When it's our building that may be sold or torn down, we easily forget the wise words of the nun, "Buildings are inanimate and we can't afford to keep them when they are no longer of use to us." Her values were in right order. People come before buildings, and the ongoing mission of Christ's church stands above everything else.

Learning to Assess

In evangelism, we need faith, courage, and a willingness to take risks and try things at which others may shake their heads. At the same time, we need to pray for wisdom to honestly assess what's doable and what isn't, what's in line with biblical goals and the example of Christ's apostles and what isn't. When the Holy Spirit sends us warnings, often by way of advice from workers with more experience, we should be humble enough to take the message seriously, reassess, and save ourselves grief later on.

The lesson I learned from my work on old fishing boats was this:

assess carefully whether a particular boat can be restored to usefulness, and don't ignore the observations of your friends. I realize now that I was guided too much by emotions. While it is true that some old boats can be restored and kept in service, others cannot, and I needed to learn to assess them properly.

America today is experiencing an unprecedented surge in immigration from almost all parts of the world. Many of the immigrants are Christians, and they are positioned to evangelize fellow immigrants. They need buildings where they can worship in their own language and in cultural styles to which they are accustomed. When church buildings still in good condition can be sold or given to immigrant congregations that need them, God be praised! That too, is an act of evangelism.

For Reflection, Discussion, and Action

1. *Name some churches that have shut down. What led to their closure? What was done with the buildings?*
2. *How can church leaders assess the value of remaining in a community when membership is declining to the point where key functions of the church are breaking down?*
3. *List the principles that should guide the transfer of church property. Should it be the best price, theological similarity, or the new owners' potential for ministry in community?*

Chapter 12

Always Keep a Fishing Pole Handy

Among the things I learned from my fisherman grandfather was that a serious fisher always keeps a fishing pole handy. "You never know when you'll have a chance to fish," he told me, "and you don't want to be caught unprepared." Stored in my memory are the rods and lures he kept in the trunk of his car. Grandpa always had his eyes open for a stream or lake where he might take a few casts.

Grandpa's travels were relatively limited in scope, while mine have been global. Yet his advice has stayed with me wherever I've gone. Years ago I purchased a "travel" rod and reel that fit into my suitcase. They've travelled with me in large airliners and little Cessna's and to more lakes and rivers than I can recount. I haven't used them on every trip, but I've always had them ready just the same. As Grandpa told me, you never know when you'll have a chance to fish.

Always Be Ready

Readiness to witness for Jesus at any time and under all circumstances is basic to Christian discipleship. Opportunities often come along when we least expect them. Let me illustrate this.

It was a hot Sunday afternoon in Colombo, Sri Lanka. I had preached twice that morning, and I needed a nap. I assumed no one would disturb me, so I stretched out on the bed and fell asleep. But you guessed it—the doorbell rang. Frankly I was in a grumpy mood as I stumbled toward the door. I didn't feel like talking to anyone about anything!

I opened the door, and to my surprise a middle-aged man was standing there. He said his name was Gogerly. I had seen him several times in the neighborhood, but today he looked different. His eyes were wild. I'd heard that he was a heavy drinker, but he seemed sober. He was obviously very troubled.

I invited him to sit down on the porch, and he promptly began to pour out his troubles. He had lost his job (probably because of drinking), the family had run out of food, and his children were hungry. His wife was pregnant. He admitted he sometimes abused her and she was at the point of leaving him. The man's sense of failure and hopelessness seemed overwhelming. "Why did you come here?" I asked. He hesitated. Like a trapped animal, his eyes darted in different directions. He mumbled something I couldn't pick up. Then he said plainly, "I was on my way to commit suicide but a voice inside me said, 'Try going to that house. Maybe they will help. Give yourself one last chance. So here I am.' "

"I'll help your family," I told him. "Your children will have food tonight. But helping you is more than I can do."

He looked bewildered.

"Only God can help you," I went on. "You're in a position the Bible calls 'perishing.' It's a bad position to be in. Your record is bad and your heart is bad. But the good news is that God sent Jesus to save people like you."

I picked up the Bible on the table and read John 3:16 to him. Then I asked him to read it aloud, and he did. "Do you see the word perishing?" I asked. "The only help I have for you is Jesus."

His head went down, and I continued: "You have to put all your faith in Jesus Christ. Not in me, not in yourself. Just Jesus."

"You must also do what the Bible calls 'repent.' It means you have to tell God you're a poor lost sinner. Your record is bad and your heart is bad. You have to say a big 'no' to your old way of life. Then surrender everything to Jesus and ask him to take charge. He's the only hope I can offer you. Without Jesus you're lost."

I let the words sink in. Then I quietly asked him, "What do you want to do?"

He sank to the floor like a lead sinker. He was doubled up, with his forehead almost on the hard floor. His shoulders heaved.

Sobbing, he pleaded with Jesus to save him. He confessed more things than I care to remember. We prayed together, and when finally we were finished, there was a puddle of tears on the floor where he had been kneeling.

His conversion apparently was genuine. He went home to his family and begged their forgiveness. My wife and I helped the family temporarily, and Gogerly found a job. He stopped drinking and joined a church. The last time I saw his family, they looked happy and well-fed.

What began with an irritating interruption to what I had hoped would be an afternoon nap ended with a father saved and a family rescued from abuse and poverty. It turned out to be what we sometimes call a "divine appointment." By God's grace, I was ready when the man came to my door.

In 1 Peter 3:15, the Bible instructs us, "Always be prepared to give an answer to everyone who asks you to give the reason for the hope you have. . . ."

The Reason for Our Hope

The world is filled with people without God and without hope (Eph. 2:12). But as Christ's followers we are people with hope. Even when times are hard, we can testify that life has meaning and something better awaits us beyond. We have hope because God through the blood of Christ has drawn us near to himself and given us hope (Eph. 2:13). Our witness is all about hope. "Christ died for sins once for all, the righteous for the unrighteous, to bring you to God . . ." (1 Pet. 3:18).

Here lies the great need of so many people. On the surface they may enjoy good things. But their lives are essentially empty. They live only for today, and sooner or later their inner hopelessness becomes evident.

The Bible says to us: offer people hope! Tell them of the glory of God and his saving love revealed in Jesus Christ. Don't gloss over their sins or muffle God's law. Tell them straight out they're perishing. But tell them, too, that perishing people who repent and come to God through Jesus will be forgiven and their lives transformed. There is room in the Father's house for everyone who comes.

Always have a fishing pole handy, my grandpa said, because you never know when or where you'll have an opportunity to fish. For fishers of souls that means to be always ready to offer hope—the hope of the gospel, the only hope there is.

For Reflection, Discussion, and Action

1. *Think about experiences you've had of unexpected opportunities to lead people to Christ. How did you respond to the opportunities and how would you want to do things differently next time.*
2. *Suggest three or four ways in which we can prepare ourselves to witness effectively when God sends special opportunities our way.*
3. *Our readiness to lead others to the source of hope in Jesus is affected by our own relationship to him. How strong is that relationship? Identify two or three indicators that you are growing steadily in fellowship with God.*

CHAPTER 13

NO FISHING

It's a familiar sign in some places, "No Fishing!" Maybe the sign is there because the area is private property and the owners want the fish for themselves. Or, the owners have learned from experience that some outsiders leave a mess to clean up. Maybe the water is polluted, and eating the fish might endanger someone's health. Whatever the reason for the sign, its message is clear. Stay out! If you want to fish, go elsewhere. You aren't to fish in these waters.

There are governments that prohibit Christians from fishing for converts in their countries. They prohibit missionaries from entering their borders, they outlaw Bibles and religious literature, shut down churches, and block Christian radio and television programs. In the twentieth century, communist countries like China and the Soviet Union opposed all forms of Christian evangelism. Their borders were tightly closed to missionaries. More recently, we've come to realize how violent the opposition to the gospel can be in Muslim areas.

Wherever freedom of religion and freedom of speech are denied by the state or infringed upon by local groups, signs tell Christians, "No Fishing Here." Severe punishments can be imposed on anyone caught spreading the gospel and also on the converts they have made. The gravity of the reprisals raises serious questions both for those who evangelize and for their converts.

TO OBEY THE SIGNS OR NOT?

In parts of the world where severe penalties may be imposed on evangelists and new believers, the issue of whether to fish or not to fish is a serious matter. Let's look at it, first, from the side of the evangelists and missionaries. Their call is from God and their burden is for the millions of people cut off from hearing the gospel. What should they do? On the one hand, the Bible teaches that Christians should respect and obey the government (Rom. 13:1). But does that apply to laws that flatly contradict what the Bible teaches and Jesus has explicitly commanded? Jesus said, "Go and preach the gospel to the whole world" (Mark 16:15), but certain governments say, "No, you can't preach it here." What is the right response to such conflicting orders? Is there a higher law to which to appeal?

The New Testament itself provides the answer. The two apostles, Peter and John, were forbidden by the authorities in Jerusalem to preach or teach in the name of Jesus. Their response was: "Judge for yourselves whether it is right in God's sight to obey you rather than God. For we cannot help speaking about what we have seen and heard" (Acts 4:19–20). Then they went on witnessing.

Now, let's consider the question of whether to fish or not to fish from the side of the people who are converted to faith in Christ and because of their conversion suffer severe reprisals. In many places young Christians are being persecuted right now, and the threat of persecution is a major obstacle to more people becoming Christians. It takes a lot of courage to step forward for Christ when it may cost you your family, your job, and maybe your life.

In Asia, I once baptized a convert from Buddhism whose brothers threatened to kill her if she was baptized. The woman knew that her brothers meant what they said. Yet she trusted God to protect her and came forward for baptism. In another part of the world I've known converts from Islam who lost their homes, their children, and all their possessions when they decided to follow Jesus and be baptized. The newly baptized sometimes disappear, and their bodies are found days later with their throats cut.

Such things are ugly and painful to think about. Yet they must be addressed because they are happening more frequently than ever before. Fishing for souls is increasingly dangerous, both for those who carry the gospel into forbidden territory and for those who receive it. We owe them our prayers, and we also need to do some personal introspection. For so long it's been easy for those in the West to say, "I want to be a fisher for Christ." But do we realize how dangerous such fishing can be? Are we willing to risk scorn and ridicule, beatings and imprisonment, loss of family, jobs, and maybe our lives for the sake of Christ and the gospel? Think about it.

A "Code of Conduct" for Seeking Converts

There are calls today for a common code of conduct in mission work and agreed-upon guidelines for winning converts. Such calls are made in response to charges by some Hindus, Buddhists, and Muslims that Christians use material enticements to gain converts. Increasingly, the word "proselytism," with negative connotations, is used in place of evangelism. This places Christians in a difficult position, because any act of kindness can bring charges that they are employing devious means to attract converts. Deeds that Christians regard as normal acts of love and mercy, such as helping provide food and medications, are interpreted as "bait" for catching people for the purpose of making them Christians.

Admittedly, mistakes are made in the name of missions and evangelism, and perhaps some sort of ethical code might be helpful. But I would urge caution. Don't let the enemies of evangelism promote the notion that evangelism is mostly aggressive, obnoxious proselytism. If a code is developed, make sure it's in tune with Scripture. Keep in mind the example of Christ and the apostles. Bear in mind that the kind of evangelism that pleases God and receives his blessing flows out of sincere love toward the people being addressed. Love is gentle and employs no force. Material and sensual incentives have no place in biblical evangelism.

The value of laying out an ethical code in evangelism is not primarily to avoid criticism and opposition, but to avoid dishonoring Christ and disobeying his will. Opposition won't disappear no matter how careful we are. Jesus was without sin, yet his enemies slandered him even while he hung on the cross. Only the Spirit of God can convict sinners that Jesus is Lord, the gospel is true, and they must repent.

Until that happens, they'll keep putting up signs that say, "No Fishing."

For Reflection, Discussion, and Action

1. *Why do some nations oppose mission work and the preaching of the gospel within their borders?*
2. *What kinds of opposition to missions and evangelism do we find in the New Testament? What kinds of opposition are occurring now?*
3. *If Jesus says, "go," and certain countries say, "no," who do we obey? On what basis should the decision be made? What may be the consequences of the decision? Are we willing to pay the price?*

Chapter 14

The Anti~Fishing Crowd

There is an anti-fishing movement composed of well-meaning people who argue that fishing is morally wrong because it inflicts pain on fish. On this basis they rule out all forms of fishing, whether it's commercial fishing for food or recreational fishing for fun.

In addressing this issue I wish to affirm immediately that as Christians we should respect all forms of life. The Bible makes it clear that animals and fish were created by God for a purpose, and they should be neither abused or wasted. For that reason, I support efforts to protect whales and other endangered species against overfishing and anything that threatens their survival.

Furthermore, I believe that it is morally wrong to inflict unnecessary pain and suffering on any living creature. If I thought that catching fish fell into that category, I would put away my rods and tackle. Neurological research shows that fish do not suffer pain in the way humans think of pain. Fish brains are so small that it is highly unlikely that fish experience any pain at all.

The point needs to be made clear. The anti-fishing crowd is well organized and increasingly vocal, and its leaders claim to stand on high moral ground when they call for a halt to fishing. They aim to put fishers like myself in an awkward position, and we need to make our defense loud and clear. While we may respect the anti-fishing crowd for their noble intentions, we must not fall overboard when they voice their mistaken ideas.

Jesus, a Fisher?

Let's take the case for-or-against fishing to Jesus. Jesus understood the nature of fish better than anyone else, and he knew all about fishing. The gospels contain some fifty references to fishing, fishing nets, and fishing boats. Jesus called commercial fishers to become his disciples, and he never implied that the profession by which they made their living was immoral. On the contrary, Luke 5 tells us that on the occasion of calling his disciples to follow him, Jesus used his power to cause a large number of fish to be caught. If catching fish were immoral, would Jesus have done this?

On another occasion, Jesus instructed Peter to go to the lake, cast a line, and open the mouth of the first fish he caught. In the fish's mouth Peter would find a coin, and with the coin he could pay the temple tax that both Peter and Jesus owed (Matt. 17:27). If catching fish were against God's will, would Jesus have given such orders to his disciple? John 21 tells us that after Jesus had arisen and appeared to his disciples, the disciples decided to go fishing. They fished all night but caught nothing. Early in the morning, Jesus stood on the shore and called out to them: "Friends, haven't you any fish?" "No," they answered. "Throw your net on the right side of the boat and you will find some," Jesus said.

The disciples did what Jesus commanded with the result that the catch of fish was so great they were unable to haul in the net. Moreover, when the disciples landed their boats, they found that Jesus had a fire burning with fish on it. "Bring some of the fish you have just caught," said Jesus, and "come and have breakfast."

We can only conclude from this that if Jesus were here today, he would have no part in the anti-fishing movement. John 1:3 says that through Jesus all things were made, and "all things" includes fish. Jesus knew more about fish than anyone else. He knew why fish were created, the purpose of a fish's life, and he respected it. At the same time, he himself caught fish and prepared a meal of fish for his disciples. Keep that in mind the next time you meet someone who is opposed to fishing.

The Anti-Evangelism Crowd

Far more serious than the anti-fishing movement is the growing opposition to evangelism. Universalists, as they are traditionally called, insist that God's grace is the same for everyone universally, and whatever Christ did to save some he did for everyone. Therefore, in the end, all will be saved regardless of their religion.

Universalists today often represent themselves as "pluralists." Pluralists maintain that there is one God and he works in saving ways through all religions—Hinduism, Buddhism, Islam, and all the rest. What is important, say pluralists, is that people be sincere about their faith and try their best to fulfill its demands. Every religion, runs their argument, is valid for the people who embrace it and find it satisfying, and no single religion should be regarded as the only true and saving faith.

Given these views, it comes as no surprise that religious pluralists have no sympathy for Christian evangelism. As far as pluralists are concerned, evangelists and missionaries are nothing more than narrow-minded bigots who, by their activity, insult the followers of other religions, and provoke hostility and even violence. If we want peace in the world, they say, we must affirm the equal value of all religions, and that involves putting a stop to evangelism and mission work.

Anti-evangelism attitudes are strong in parts of Europe where, not long ago, churches sent large numbers of missionaries. But they don't do that anymore, for wherever pluralism spreads it is the kiss of death to missions. Now pluralism is gaining ground in North American schools, in the media, and in some churches. On many campuses, for anyone to profess openly that Jesus is the only way to the Father invites verbal abuse and intimidation. Strangely, Muslims and other religionists are increasingly bold in asserting their faith and what it requires, while most Christians remain silent. Whether their silence is due to cordiality or cowardice remains to be seen.

Wherever religious pluralism gains ground, support for evangelism fades, and other causes, like protecting the environment, replace it. Some of these causes have merit, but they fail to address the issue the Bible focuses on most, which is the reconciliation of sinners to God through the saving work of Jesus Christ. Regrettably, in some religious circles there is more interest in saving certain species of fish than supporting the saving of souls.

For Reflection, Discussion, and Action

1. *How important is it to insist that Christ is the one and only Savior? Why can't we "give in a little" for the sake of cordial relations and peace in the world?*
2. *Explain what you would do if on Easter Sunday the pastor of your church preached on highway safety?*

Chapter 15

Catch 'em, Clean 'em, Eat 'em

I grew up during the Great Depression of the 1930s, followed by World War II with its rationing of meat, butter, and gasoline. During the Depression years most people couldn't afford meat, and during the war they couldn't get it. So I learned at an early age to regard fish as valuable food and something never to be wasted. We fished a lot for pan fish in those days, because they were easy to catch and made for good eating.

We followed a set of rules that I call a Good Fishers Code, and it went like this: In fisher's language, first you gotta catch 'em. This means learning a basic set of skills designed to catch pan fish, skills such as how to:

- handle a pole with a hook and linc,
- select a sinker of the right weight and attach it to the line at the right place,
- adjust a bobber according to the depth of the water,
- bait the hook with an earthworm or minnow, cast it out, and wait patiently for a fish to nibble,
- watch the bobber every minute; when it wiggles, goes under, or runs away, raise the tip of the pole; and if all goes well, you will have caught a fish.

Next, you gotta clean 'em. At this point some would-be fishers lose interest in fishing. Quite frankly, cleaning fish is a messy job. Nobody masters the art of cleaning fish without getting some cuts and scratches. I learned to clean perch, bluegills, sunfish, and crappies before I had finished second grade, and so did my sons. (My daughters got their brothers to do it for them.) Now I watch my grandsons cleaning and filleting fish faster than I ever did.

Sometimes when the fish were biting really well, we'd fish until after dark, and when we came home we were tired. That's when the second rule of the Good Fishers Code was put to the test. Could we leave the fish in a bucket of water and clean 'em in the morning? Or do we have to clean 'em now? There was just one answer. We clean 'em now. Our family's work ethic did not allow wasting food or putting off unpleasant tasks, not even in good economic times. "Fish," my dad would say, "are God's creatures, and God meant them for food" (Gen. 9:2–3). That meant their meat must not be left to spoil. So we lighted a couple of kerosene lamps and cleaned 'em.

Then comes rule number 3, you gotta eat 'em. Some people don't like to eat fish, at least not home-cooked fish that the fishers in the family bring home. But in my family, none of us got away with that. "You caught 'em and cleaned 'em," my mother would say, "and I've fried them in the kitchen. Now, we're all going to eat 'em." We did, and in the eating we learned to like them.

The Code Applied to Evangelism

The three steps of the Good Fishers Code apply to evangelism, and here is how. First, we "catch" sinners by proclaiming the gospel to whomever the Holy Spirit draws to listen. There is no other way, for as the Bible says, "Faith comes by hearing the message, and and the message is heard through the word of Christ" (Rom. 10:17). The gospel is plain enough: Christ died for sinners, and by the grace of God all who repent and believe in him receive complete forgiveness and the free gift of eternal life (John 3:16).

Some Christians excuse themselves by saying that "catching" isn't their spiritual gift. That excuse sounds phony to me. Didn't Jesus say to Simon Peter, "Don't be afraid; from now on you will catch men" (Luke 5:10)? If we don't learn to catch 'em, we shouldn't be surprised when our churches consist mostly of "old-timers," as so many churches do.

The second step requires long, hard work. The "caught" must be "cleaned" of the ways of sin in which they previously walked, and taught to walk in the new and righteous way of obedience to God. The cleaning process lasts a lifetime and isn't finished until the believer arrives in heaven. But it must be started as soon as the heart surrenders to Christ and never be allowed to slack off.

Christ commanded us to "make disciples," not momentary "converts." Disciples are men and women, boys and girls, who are baptized in the name of God the Father, the Son, and the Holy Spirit and spend their lives seeking to obey everything the Lord commands in his Word.

For this to take place, it's important to become part of a Bible-teaching church. It must be a church whose members are open to receiving newly caught "fish" and, working together with the Word and the Spirit, "cleaning 'em." Some churches do not care to embrace new people who still have the "smell" of the world's dead fish about them. They expect new members to be clean from the outset. But evangelism doesn't work that way. First you catch 'em and then you go about cleaning 'em. Otherwise, you're left literally with a "mess of fish."

You may be wondering about the third step. In terms of our paradigm, how do we "eat" new believers? The answer is: we do it by gladly receiving them as newborn babes in Christ, and incorporating them into the church, the body of believers.

New Christians need guidance and encouragement from godly pastors and elders. Over time, every corner of their lives will have to be examined, cleansed, and transformed. This requires plenty of "scrubbing" by the Holy Spirit from the inside and the ministry of the Word through pastors and Christian friends from the outside.

Sad to say, some churches are so ingrown along family lines and bound by traditions, or so racially or culturally exclusive, that anyone who's different feels excluded. Such churches need lessons in how to fish for folks of different kinds.

There's a story I love to tell because it illustrates much of what we've been discussing. Bullheads are probably the ugliest fish in the lake, and hardly anyone wants to catch them. Not only do they look ugly, bullheads have sharp horns on either side of their mouths that can cut your fingers and cause infections. Most fishers, if they hook a bullhead, would rather cut the line and drop the fish back in the water rather than mess with it in the boat. But we had a neighbor who loved to catch bullheads because he knew how to handle them and fix them for eating. His secret was to smoke them! He'd turned a big steel drum into a smoking oven, and when he smoked a rack of bullheads they came out tasting like smoked salmon.

I leave it to you readers to make the applications. Think about it.

For Reflection, Discussion, and Action

1. *What is the only legitimate "bait" to use in evangelism? What are things we can do so that the "fish" and the "bait" come in contact?*
2. *Does your church regularly receive and effectively enfold people with little or no Christian background? Have some started, but left for another church? Why?*
3. *How will you apply the Good Fishers Code to yourself and your church in the next six months?*

Chapter 16

Small Hook Evangelism

"If you want to catch bluegills, use small hooks, either size number 8 or number 10." That was the advice a man gave me years ago. Time after time I had watched him catch more bluegills than any of the rest of us. What was his secret? One day he told me: "Use small hooks."

For pan fish, I had always used the standard size number 6. It worked fairly well, yet that other man always out-fished me. I took his advice and started using smaller hooks. It worked, and I've used number 8s ever since. I've passed on the lesson to my children and grandchildren, and it works for them, too.

Besides using a small hook, I discovered that you have to avoid putting on too much bait. Big, fat worms attract a lot of fish and bring bites, but not many fish end up in the bucket. Fish are smart, and when they see a juicy worm or a fat cricket they nibble away at it without getting hooked. You may think it's fun to feed fish, but that isn't what fishers are on the lake for.

Evangelistic Preaching

One of the most common mistakes preachers fresh out of seminary make is to overload their messages with scholarly theology. Now, don't get me wrong. Theological truth is important, and every good sermon contains enough divine truth for the Holy Spirit to germinate in hearers' hearts. But too much at one time sends people away confused, maybe never to return.

I speak from (painful) experience about this. I've preached for over fifty years, in thirty-five different countries, and much of my preaching was evangelistic in nature. But I admit that oftentimes I overloaded my message with things that my listeners weren't prepared to understand or respond to. I must repent from fishing for men unwisely.

For example, I was in Uganda, East Africa, toward the end of the terrible civil war that tore the country apart. On a particular Sunday morning, I was surprised to be invited to preach at an army barracks to a crowd of Ugandan soldiers, many of them Muslims. Their commanding officer had recently become a Christian, and he was so excited about Jesus Christ that he wanted the men under his command to hear the gospel, whether they wanted to or not. He ordered all the soldiers to the service where I was to preach.

I felt tension in the air as the soldiers filed in, each of them carrying his weapon. The soldiers in the front row set down their machine guns mounted on tripods pointing toward me! I knew full well that the Muslims among them had been taught that Jesus did not die on the cross. Yet God led me to preach on that very subject, the cross of Christ and what it means.

Since dawn that morning I had been seeking divine guidance as to how to address so controversial a subject. Complex theories about the atonement would not do. I had to make the message of "Christ and him crucified" as clear as possible. I wanted every soldier to grasp the central truths of the gospel and then leave it to the Holy Spirit to produce conviction, repentance, and faith.

At the close of the service, the soldiers shouldered their weapons and left, and I was left wondering what they were thinking. Did I bring them face-to-face with Jesus? Or did my message contain words and ideas too hard to understand? My role was over as far as that group of Ugandans were concerned. I could only leave the follow-up to the Holy Spirit and local Christians. Eternity will tell whether I served the Lord well that day or not.

The Wisdom of Watchman Nee

Watchman Nee (his Chinese name was Ni To-sheng) was one of the great evangelists of the twentieth century. Many of his sermons were taken down in shorthand and later published as books. Nee began an indigenous Christian movement in China that brought thousands of Chinese people to salvation. In 1952, he was arrested by the Communists for his religious activities. He spent the last twenty years of his life in prison, where he died in 1972. The movement he began, however, did not die out despite persecution. It continues growing to this day and with the same basic earmarks that Nee gave it: Keep your witness simple, introduce Jesus as best you can, and trust the Holy Spirit.

In his book What Shall This Man Do? Nee urged all believers to consider themselves unpaid workers for the gospel whose homes were places of prayer and witness. In regard to witnessing, Nee emphasized simplicity. He said we should ask only that inquirers approach Christ with an honest desire to meet him. The first step of salvation is not a bucket full of knowledge, but meeting Jesus. Instruction should follow, but without personal encounter, little else matters.

Watchman Nee illustrated his point by referring to three people in the gospels: the dying thief, who in his final hour turned to Jesus and simply asked to be remembered when Jesus came into his kingdom; the bleeding woman who reached out to touch Jesus; and the publican in Jesus' parable who cried out for mercy. Each one in a particular way came in touch with God and was saved.

All across China and in many other parts of the world, hundreds of thousands are being touched by Jesus in much the same way as the dying thief, the bleeding woman, and the guilt-ridden publican. They may not own a Bible, or even be able to read. But the one needful thing they know: Jesus is a friend of sinners, and they can trust him with their needs.

Are Our Fishhooks Too Big?

With roughly half the population of North America unchurched and unsaved, an enormous mission field lies at our doorstep. However, what bewilders me is that despite all the Bibles, religious books, magazines, and instruction materials available, so many of us are grossly ineffective in basic one-on-one evangelism. In contrast, in some other parts of the world where Christians have less training and minimal resources, believers are winning souls and multiplying churches. I ask: What's our problem?

Are the "hooks" we use too large? Have we overloaded our witness to the point of ineffectiveness? I admit that I often have made that mistake, and I doubt that I stand alone. Sometimes education has gotten in my way and I've had to remind myself that effective witnessing does not require that we have answers to every question. It all starts with leading unsaved people to meet Jesus, the friend of sinners, and trusting the Holy Spirit to carry on from there. I believe that it's precisely at the starting point that we need to use smaller hooks! Just make sure that the hooks are sharp and you know what to do when fish bite.

For Reflection, Discussion, and Action

1. *Describe the time when you met Jesus and took him to be your friend for life.*
2. *What are you doing regularly to grow in truth, knowledge, holiness, and witness?*
3. *Are you ready and willing to make a pledge to cast a bite-sized bit of gospel truth to one unsaved person per week for the next two months?*

Chapter 17

While Little Boys Are Fishin'

The late George Younce sang a song entitled "God Loves to Talk to Little Boys While They're Fishing." Boys, the song goes, who listen to God when they're fishing will hear him when he calls to fish for men.[1]

Boys have learned fishing from their fathers and grandfathers for centuries. The Bible tells us that four of Jesus' disciples—Peter, Andrew, James, and John—were sons of fishermen. The boys grew up in a small town on the shore of the Sea of Galilee, and catching fish was the way their families made a living. From childhood they'd learned about fishing boats, nets, and where and when to find fish. They probably learned also that good fishermen don't talk much while they're fishing.

One day, Jesus called the four of them to follow him and he'd teach them to "catch men." By this, Jesus meant to say, I'll teach you to evangelize people. Fishing is a paradigm for evangelism, and these men had learned lessons in childhood that they would now apply to a new and higher calling.

Ah, childhood memories. On a wall in our den I have mounted two casting rods that date back to the 1930s. The rods are made of split bamboo, and each has a reel filled with black braided casting line. One rod was made by the famous Heddon company and the reel by Shakespeare. The other rod was also made by Heddon and the reel by South Bend. Why do I treasure these two old rods and reels? Because the one belonged to my father and the other to my grandfather. When

1 *Gaither Recordings,* "A Tribute to George Younce: God Loves to Talk to Little Boys While They're Fishing." *Spring House Publications, Inc., 2005.*

I was a boy and I saw my father or grandfather bring out their rods, it meant they were going fishing. Provided that I promised not to scare the fish away by talking too much, they'd take me along. Of all my childhood memories, the sweetest are those of fishing on a lake with Dad and Granddad, whether we caught a lot of fish or not.

In the annals of missionary history, few names are greater than that of Samuel M. Zwemer. He spent decades witnessing to Muslims from Arabia to India to China, and from North Africa to the southern tip of that great continent. He published more than fifty books meant to inform people in the West about Islam and awaken churches to send missionaries. Zwemer is rightly called the "apostle to Islam."[2] Yet the price he had to pay was high—primitive conditions, life-threatening diseases, the death of two young children due to dysentery, and fanatical opposition. He "fished" far and wide, seeking Muslims, as he put it, "wherever he might find them."

Samuel Zwemer's book, The Moslem Doctrine of God, was published in 1905. Samuel dedicated the book to his father and placed the following words on the title page:

To My Beloved Father, Adrian Zwemer

Yet most I thank thee, not for any deed,

But for the sense thy living self did breed

That Fatherhood is at the great world's core. [3]

Samuel Zwemer's profound analysis of the Muslim conception of Allah, where the Fatherhood of God is denied, turned his thoughts to his own father, Adrian Zwemer. From childhood, Samuel had learned important truths about his heavenly Father by what he had seen and felt in his earthly father.

Adrian Zwemer was a faithful husband, father, and pastor of a country church. I can't prove that he ever took Samuel fishing. But

2 *Kenneth Scott Latourette,* Introduction to J. Christy Wilson, Apostle to Islam: A Biography of Samuel M. Zwemer. *Grand Rapids, MI:Baker Book House, 1953: 4.*

3 *Samuel M. Zwemer,* The Moslem Doctrine of God: An Essay on the Character and Attributes of Allah According to the Koran and Orthodox Tradition. *New York: American Tract Society, 1905.*

since they lived in Michigan where there's an abundance of lakes and streams, it's a safe assumption they went fishing. What we know for certain is that Samuel learned in early boyhood to listen to God's voice, and when later God called him to "fish for men," he answered. The patience and persistence that boys learn by fishing characterized Samuel's ministry throughout his life.

Samuel never mentioned any material things his father gave him. Instead, he praised his father for his character, his "living self" that was to Samuel a glimpse of the nature and heart of God. Later, when he was in college, Samuel was struck by the absence of God's Fatherhood in Islam and his passion was kindled to bring the gospel to Muslims. When God said to him, "It's time to fish for men," Samuel was ready.

Two of the fishermen whom Jesus called to follow him were James and John, sons of Zebedee and Salome. After James and John left to follow Jesus, Zebedee kept the family fishing business going. Salome on the other hand, was among the women who accompanied Jesus and the disciples, supporting them financially and assisting in their work. Salome was at Calvary when Jesus was crucified, and on resurrection morning she was among the women who came to the tomb intending to anoint Jesus' body (Mark 15:40–41; 16:1).

Both Salome and Zebedee believed in Jesus and the importance of his work, and when Jesus called their sons to leave the family's business, they raised no objection (Matt. 4:21–22). Zebedee kept fishing while his wife Salome accompanied the disciples. Serving Jesus was for them a family affair.

Children raised in homes where they regularly listen to God's Word in church, at family table, and sometimes at a lake, learn spiritual values that shape their hearts and lives. After Samuel Zwemer had decided to become a missionary, he learned to his surprise that before he was born his mother had dedicated him to the Lord for missionary service. Having ingested missions with his mother's milk, it's no surprise that he said "yes" when God said, "It's time to fish for men."[4]

4 *Ibid.*

For Reflection, Discussion, and Action

1. *If your son or daughter tells you that God has called them to serve him in missions, how will you feel about it?*
2. *What is it about our heavenly Father that your children learn by living with you?*
3. *Have you taken a boy or girl fishing lately? Do it soon.*

Chapter 18

A Rod in the Box and a Broken Net

A friend at church gave me a surprising gift, an exquisite, handmade, bamboo fly rod. He had gotten it many years ago from a neighbor that was moving an elderly grandmother to a nursing home. The rod is in mint condition and rests serenely in a thirty-four-inch wooden box with small brass hinges and clasps. Made long before World War II, it appears never to have been used, in fact, never taken out of the box.

To collectors and connoisseurs of fine fishing tackle, this rod is a prize. What skilled craftsmanship went into rods like this! It probably took more than one hundred hours to make it. An appraiser estimated its value at several thousand dollars. Yet to me, the rod has one serious problem: it has lain there in its box for more than seventy-five years, never catching any fish. It shows no signs of wear or tear, no fish scales or smears of dried blood. It was made for fishing, not staying in a box. Now its delicate strands of split bamboo are so dry and brittle that even a small trout might break the tip.

Churches Like the Rod in the Box

When it comes to evangelism, churches have two major problems. Problem number one is their similarity to the rod in the box. They're high quality, teach the right things, own beautiful buildings, offer splendid music, use the latest in equipment, and have marvelous programs to keep everyone busy. But their fatal flaw is that they don't fish for sinners lost in the world. Their ministries are mostly designed for people who've been Christians for generations and are comfortable "in the box." Their nonevangelistic ethos is so ingrained that they couldn't catch fish if they tried. Like my old rod, they're brittle, entrenched in their ways, and incapable of engaging the hurly-burly world of outreach.

Broken Nets

The second major problem found in many churches relates to fishing nets and the failure to maintain nets well. The Bible mentions several times that Jesus' fishermen-disciples spent time cleaning and repairing their nets. Mending nets is dull work, and fishers prefer to be out on the water lowering and raising nets and pulling in a catch of fish. But if nets are not maintained in first-rate condition, the end results will be disappointing.

Similarly, churches need leaders who continually evaluate and monitor the spiritual health of their congregations. Good maintenance involves teaching and defending sound doctrine, correcting weaknesses, ministering to people at all stages of spiritual development, and repairing the damage that Satan causes.

I know fishers who, whenever they go fishing, simply toss their gear into the back of a pickup, and off they go. Later, they wonder why their rods are damaged and the reels don't work. They ignore the simple fact that rods, reels, and other gear need to be carefully maintained or they'll cause problems when you least expect it. Let me illustrate this mistake from my own experience.

One weekend my wife and I had as our guest a Nigerian pastor who was studying in the United Sates. He had never gone fishing. Seeing that we live on a lake he asked me to take him fishing because he wanted to bring his wife a fresh fish. At the crack of dawn the next morning I loaded up my pontoon boat, and we headed for a spot on the lake where large mouth bass are often found. I had taken along casting rods, bass lures, a can of big, fat night crawlers, and as usual my long-handled net.

But that morning, the fish weren't biting, and my Nigerian friend was disappointed. As the time approached when we had to quit, I said,

"One more cast." You can guess what happened: Bang—I got a strike, and I knew immediately that it was a much bigger fish than a bass. The line on my reel was only six-pound test, so I fought the fish slowly. It swung around the boat, dove to the bottom, and played all the tricks big fish know about. Gradually the fish got tired, and when it came to the surface we were surprised at its size. It was a northern pike more than a yard long and weighing at least ten or twelve pounds. My friend was in ecstasy, and out of the corner of my eye I saw him dancing, Nigerian style, at the other end of the boat. The problem for me was that I had to handle both the pole and the net alone.

I worked the pike until it appeared worn out, and I drew him alongside the boat. Holding the rod in one hand and the net in the other, I reached down and scooped it into the net. I had him, or so I thought. From head to tail the fish was in the net, with its long body bent in a U-shape. That's when the fish gave a jerk, stretched itself out full length, and its head tore a hole in the net. In a flash it was back in the lake. Now I had a bigger problem because the fish was still hooked and the line ran through the hoop of the net. I now had to manage the net, fight the fish, hold onto the rod, and crank the reel.

To keep the story short, I clenched the net's handle between my knees and gradually cranked the reel until the fish was directly below me. I knew the line wasn't strong enough to lift a fish that size up the side and into the boat. My only chance was to reach down and take hold of the wire leader, and just maybe I'd be able to lift him aboard. Well, the plan didn't work. A moment before my hand reached the leader the line snapped, and the pike was gone. My Nigerian friend was almost in tears. He'd been so excited thinking he'd have a couple of nice fillets to take to his wife. It was all due to my failure to properly maintain the net, one I'd used for a couple of years without testing its condition.

My mistake was analogous to the error made by church leaders who don't monitor closely enough the spiritual growth of their members. One of the lessons I learned from my father was the importance of knowing parishioners personally and carefully monitoring their spiritual health and growth. My father exemplified the type of pastor that some people criticize today, calling them "maintenance ministers" as opposed to "missional" leaders. But I learned from him that if you don't pay close attention to the spiritual health of the whole spectrum of church members, weaknesses in the net are bound to appear, and they'll cost you lost fish. Every church he served was larger and stronger when he left than when he arrived, due largely to his pastoral intuition that it's important to maintain the right balance between "catching 'em, cleaning 'em, and eating 'em."

Remember Your Baptism and Fish for Men!

In our church there is a man who years ago was a great fisherman, but now he is confined to a wheelchair. Despite this, he makes wonderful fishing rods. At the close of a recent baptismal service he wheeled himself to the front of the church and presented each of the newly baptized a fishing rod. "Remember your baptism," he said, "and fish for men!" That's it! Can't you see the angels smiling?

For Reflection, Discussion, and Action

1. *Why do some Christians "stay in the box" rather than getting out and fishing for men?*
2. *How would you describe the proper balance between casting nets and mending them?*
3. *What have you learned here that you'll put into practice?*

CHAPTER 19

PARTNERS IN OTHER BOATS

Partnerships are popular among businesses today, and they are multiplying as well within the missionary community. Mission specialists call partnerships the right paradigm for twenty-first-century missions. The old paradigm, they say, emphasized pioneering, while the new paradigm focuses on partnering. Some denominations, my own included, celebrate their "worldwide partnerships," many of them with overseas churches and some with community development organizations. In countries like India, where hundreds of indigenous missionary organizations have recently sprung up, Christians are aware that they can accomplish more through partnerships than by independent operations.

Partnerships are not a recent invention, nor are the benefits a new discovery. Luke 5:11 tells of Jesus calling his first four disciples. All of them were commercial fishers and in partnership with each other. An incident occurred one day when Jesus was preaching by the seaside to a large crowd of people. Jesus spotted two fishing boats left there by fishermen who were washing their nets. Jesus got into one of the boats and asked Peter, its owner, to put out a little from shore. The boat became Jesus' pulpit that day.

When Jesus had finished preaching, he told Peter to "put out into deep water, and let down the nets for a catch" (Luke 5:4). Peter didn't think that was a wise idea, but he and his crew did what Jesus said. To their amazement they caught such a large number of fish that their nets began to break. Rather than lose the fish, they signaled their partners in the other boat to come and help them. They came and filled both boats so full that they began to sink.

It strikes me that two different yet parallel situations are found here. On the one hand there is the large catch that made Peter seek help from partners in another boat, and on the other hand there is the current surge in global church growth that makes mission partnering the sensible way to go.

Benefits of Partnering

The first benefit of partnering is the witness it gives that Christians are not only one in the Lord, but are also united in love and service.

The second benefit is as practical as it is obvious. We can generally accomplish more when we work with partners than we can by working alone. Had the other boats not come to help, Peter's nets might have broken and the catch lost.

Third, partners encourage one another, complement each other's talents, and fill in when someone departs, becomes ill, or dies. These probably are some of the reasons why Jesus sent out the seventy "two by two" (Luke 10:1, 17), and why the apostle Paul usually traveled with one or more companions.

Let me tell a story that illustrates the importance of partnerships. I once went by canoe with three evangelists to an island off the coast of Honduras where a group of believers had asked for help. Theirs was the only church on the island, and the lady missionary who had planted the church had died. They took us to the house where the missionary had lived for sixteen years. Thick dust covered everything and bats clung to the ceiling. When we entered and light shone in through the doorway, the little creatures dove around our heads like dive-bombers. In the missionary's desk drawer, I found her handwritten journal. It covered the years she had ministered there on the island and what she had done to make it a center of outreach to small neighboring islands. The names and dates of persons baptized, children born, and funerals conducted were all recorded in the book. But the record stopped abruptly and only blank pages remained in the book. The missionary had died, leaving neither partners nor local leaders trained to replace her. She apparently had been a marvelous, hardworking soloist but a poor mission strategist.

Following her death, a small group of women kept the Sunday school going, but that was all they knew how to do. They begged us to send a worker from the mainland. They knew how to touch our hearts. As our canoe shoved off from the shore, the women led a group of children singing in Spanish, "Lord of harvest, send forth reapers." If only that dear missionary had established partnerships and trained local leaders, the story would surely have been different.

A fourth reason why partners are important lies in the fact that the work of developing churches and transforming communities involves more specialized ministries than any one group can deliver. For example, evangelists need Bibles in the local languages, which means linking up with skilled Bible translators, publishers, and distributors. In remote rural areas where nearly half the children may die before they're five, partner agencies with specialized skills and resources can drill wells to supply safe water, show local people how to build latrines, provide medical assistance, set up schools, and train teachers. In urban areas, one of the greatest needs is for partners that specialize in reaching young people for Christ. Sad to say, few churches are prepared to engage in effective ministries to young people who have little or no church background.

There is a fifth benefit, also. Having partners in the free world is a matter of survival for churches in countries where Christians are oppressed and persecution can erupt at any time. At such moments, international partners become advocates who can alert the media and pressure governments to intervene.

Cautions to Observe

Like marriage, a mission partnership should not be rushed into or expected to work smoothly without proper maintenance. Here are some pointers to observe.

First, make sure the intended partners share the same Christian convictions, can tolerate minor differences, and are united in their vision, values, and goals. Investigate these matters carefully before a partnership begins. At one stage of my ministry I was assigned to work with a partner organization that my mission board had not investigated carefully enough beforehand. It taught us some painful lessons.

Second, trust and accountability are essential in matters involving money and property. Western and non-Western churches and organizations often have different approaches to financial accountability. For that reason, I caution against sending financial support to any individual, church, or organization that is not accountable to a reliable association or umbrella organization in its own country or region.

Third, partnership relations should be reviewed periodically to determine their effectiveness. There is no sense in maintaining an ineffective partnership.

Peter, Andrew, James, and John were partners in the fishing business before they followed Jesus. They fished from separate boats, yet they helped each other effectively when needed. That is what mission partnerships are meant to do, and when the needed cautions are observed, they generally advance the gospel and benefit the workers.

For Reflection, Discussion, and Action

1. *Name some partnerships you are acquainted with and evaluate their effectiveness.*
2. *What seems to motivate go-it-alone mission operations? Under what conditions might they be advisable?*
3. *Who evaluates the effectiveness of the partnerships your church supports? Might it be time for a fresh look?*

Chapter 20

Peter's Fish

Tilapia is a wonderful fish to eat, and many restaurants in America feature tilapia on their menus. Its flesh is low-fat, sweet, and fine-textured. About the size of a large bluegill or sunfish, tilapia reproduce in large numbers and grow fast.

In Jesus' day, the Sea of Galilee was famous for its tilapia. There were hundreds of fishermen with their boats circling its shores. Today, tilapia are "aquacultured," which means they are raised in fish ponds by fish farmers. In poor countries, relief and development agencies teach local farmers how to raise tilapia as a source of food and protein for their families.

Tilapia are often called "saint Peter's fish." This refers to the story in the Bible in which Peter, the disciple of Jesus, comes to Jesus with a money problem. They don't have enough money to pay their taxes. Jesus responds to the problem in a surprising way. He tells Peter to go to the lake (commonly called the Sea of Galilee) and throw out a line, and the first fish he catches will have the tax money in its mouth (Matt. 17:27).

Can you imagine the look on Peter's face? He's incredulous! He has fished in the Sea of Galilee since he was a boy, and never has he seen a fish with a coin in its mouth. Is Jesus joking?

But Jesus is serious. He means what he told Peter to do. Dragging his feet, Peter gets his fishing tackle. He's probably mumbling to himself, "What does Jesus know about fishing? Jesus didn't grow up in a fishing boat like I did, and now he tells me to cast a line and catch a fish with money in its mouth! Who is he fooling? What kind of man am I following?"

Despite his doubts and questions, Peter goes to the lake and casts a line. Before long he catches a fish. Carefully, he takes hold of it, and with a deep breath opens the fish's mouth. Then he gasps. In the fish's mouth is a coin, a silver Greek coin worth exactly the amount needed to pay Jesus' tax and his own.

As Peter stood there staring at the fish, his faith in Jesus took a huge leap forward. That one small fish did more than cover their taxes. It served to enlarge Peter's faith in the one who had called him to become a "fisher of men." A wave of new thoughts about Jesus began to sweep over Peter's mind like a wave of the sea.

Jesus obviously possessed knowledge of a supernatural kind. He knew that this particular fish had picked up a coin from the bottom of the water and was holding it in its mouth. How did Jesus know this? To a seasoned fisher, it was beyond human explanation. In Jesus, Peter confronted what scholars call divine omniscience:God's all-encompassing knowledge, which extends even to fish in the sea.

Peter thought further. How could Jesus, while standing at a distance from the sea, not only know where this fish was but also cause the fish to swim to the exact spot where Peter was casting a line? Now Peter was confronted with what scholars call divine omnipotence, the sovereign power of God to do everything he wills to do.

Peter shivered when he thought of the person he was following. He had viewed Jesus as a great prophet and wise teacher, yet still just a man. But increasingly, Peter sensed that Jesus was more than a man. Jesus possessed powers that no mere man ever had. Only God could know what Jesus knew; only God controlled winds, waves, and fish in the sea. At the moment when Peter saw the coin in the fish's mouth, the mystery of Jesus' personhood seized him. Somehow, beyond comprehension, Jesus was both God and man. Later, Peter put his feelings into words, saying to Jesus, "You are the Christ, the Son of the living God" (Matt. 16:16). Scholars describe it as incarnation: "The Word became flesh and made his dwelling among us, we have seen his glory . . ." (John 1:14).

Peter reflected on his role as a follower of Jesus. He was to trust Jesus and do what he said. Sometimes what Jesus said seemed strange and unreasonable, like fishing for a fish with a coin in its mouth. But if Jesus was all the things Peter saw him to be, then Peter could follow him anywhere. In fact, to follow Jesus was the greatest privilege anyone could imagine. That's what the Bible teaches about discipleship. It's trusting Jesus and obeying what he commands.

What If?

What if Peter had said to himself, "What does Jesus know about catching fish? Of all the fish I've caught, I've never found a coin in any fish's mouth! I need the money, and I'll get it my way." How would the story have ended?

Or what if Peter, instead of using a simple hook and line as Jesus said, had gone to his boat, rowed out to deeper water, and let down a net for a big catch? No matter how many fish Peter might have caught, he would have missed the one fish that had all the money they needed in its mouth. Most importantly, he would have missed the revelation that unlimited knowledge and power belong to Jesus and the encouragement this gives to those who follow him.

Peter's fish will always be remembered for the lessons it teaches. Lessons such as trusting Jesus to meet your needs. Those who serve Jesus can trust him to know where the resources are and how to reach them. Trust and obey him, and be ready for surprises.

And there's the lesson of giving God the praise for every fish you catch. Ephesians 1:1–14 flows from the humble heart of a missionary, the apostle Paul, and it speaks to fishers for souls in every generation. Triune God has known from eternity every fish we catch. The Father chose them, the Son died for them, and the Spirit draws them to the gospel and regenerates them. Our role is to be fishers, God's coworkers (1 Cor. 3:9). When, someday, our fishing's done and the last tilapia is in the boat, we'll give God all the glory because we fished by his grace alone.

On a Sunday night in September 1957, I attended the commissioning service of a new missionary. If earlier that day someone would have told me that before the day was over I would be committed to a lifetime in missions and evangelism, I would have brushed the idea aside. But at exactly 7:25 p.m., while we were singing "Living for Jesus," the Lord spoke to me, I would almost say audibly. I can't recall exactly what he said, but his message was clear: Roger, I call you to become a "fisher of men."

I went home in a daze and told my wife what had happened, and we spent the night talking, praying, and some crying, too. By morning we were united in our decision. The Lord had called us and we would follow him. Half a century later we still carry on.

Remember Peter's fish! When the master fisher calls to you, fish—do it! You'll be surprised at the catch.

For Reflection, Discussion, and Action

1. Why did Jesus send Peter on such a strange fishing trip?

2. What encouragement can we get from this story?

3. Has Jesus called you? What's your answer?